# IVAN

A DARK MAFIA ROMANCE

SOPHIE LARK

# 1

## SLOANE

ST. PETERSBURG, RUSSIA

*Sometimes death lurks after them for days, weeks, or even months, waiting for their time...*

— N.B. Roberts

I stroll into the club, past the doormen who by now know me well enough to let me in with a nod. I've got my fur coat buttoned up to the neck, and my feet stuffed into some lovely new fleece-lined boots, because it's bitterly cold outside. The snow is blowing in from the west, the flakes as tiny and granular as sand, biting every inch of exposed skin.

But that's just an average November evening in St. Petersburg. It hasn't deterred the patrons of the club, who fill the expensive leather booths and especially the seats around the stage. The heat of their bodies has almost made it too warm inside. I'm eager to get to the staff room to shuck off my coat.

I've been working here six weeks, long enough to become familiar to the regulars and the other girls. It's longer than most people would have devoted to a job like this, but that's why I'm the best at what I do. I don't shirk on the details.

Even when the details are, shall we say . . . somewhat unpleasant.

I head to the change room, which is a mess of curling irons and lipstick tubes, discarded boots and glittery thongs. I open up my coat to reveal the outfit underneath, if it can be called an outfit at all—it's more like three little patches of black leather, held onto my body by elaborate, crisscrossing silver chains.

Now I have to do what all the girls have already done and exchange my nice comfy boots for a pair of awful platform heels. Then I touch up my hair and makeup. The hair is a wig. Blonde, because Yozhin exclusively likes blondes. And the makeup—smoky eyes and pouting red lips—is about ten times more than I'd usually wear.

While I'm dolling myself up, a couple more girls come in— Marta, who's from a little town in Belarus, and Angie, who's American, like me. Marta goes by the stage name Star. Angie calls herself Montana, though she's actually from Idaho. She came here as a backpacker, then started stripping once she ran out of money.

They think my name is Amanda Wallace and that I'm in a similar boat to Angie. Angie helped me pick my stage name, which is Roxie. I made sure to make friends with Angie the second I saw her, because she's exactly the type Yozhin likes: blonde, fake tits, with a sweet girl-next-door smile.

I've only got one of those things, and the hair isn't even real. But it's fooled Yozhin so far. He's paid for private dances with Angie and me every night that he's come in.

I could have done the job the first time I had him alone in the private room, but first encounters are the enemy. Yozhin's body-guards were watching us. Yozhin himself was too riled up, his hands all over me—paying too much attention to the "new girl." Even if I'd managed to slip something in his drink without anyone noticing, it would have drawn too much attention if he started foaming at the mouth within five minutes of meeting me.

Routine is what I look for. Complaisance.

That's the time to take someone. When they're perfectly comfortable and happy.

I want a man to die in front of the fire with his slippers on and his favorite cigar in his mouth.

I'm a very considerate grim reaper.

Yozhin's favorite place is probably this strip club. He certainly doesn't stop grinning from the moment he steps foot in the door. And he comes every Wednesday night, like clockwork.

If he really cared about staying alive, he wouldn't be so predictable. He also wouldn't have pissed off whoever it was that hired me.

But that's his problem, not mine.

I just give him dance after dance. I let him put his pudgy little hands all over me, until I could kill him out of pure disgust, let alone for the $50K in bitcoin wired to my account.

The men at the club aren't supposed to touch us. This is a high-end establishment, not some cheap speakeasy where the girls give out blowjobs at the tables for three thousand rubles a pop. But Yozhin is the minister of the Admiralteysky District, so there's some leeway. He's not the biggest fish to come in here, but he's important enough to get what he wants.

He gets his pick of the girls and the same VIP table every time. He orders a dozen bottles of top shelf liquor for whatever entourage he's brought along, and he's generous with his tips. And yet, apparently, someone wants him dead.

And they want it to look like an accident.

Murder is easy.

Stealth is a little harder.

Of course, I already know what I'll be using. I plan to poison him tonight, when he takes Angie and I back for a private dance.

He's an important man, so I'll have to assume that there will be an investigation, an autopsy.

There's virtually no poison that can't be discovered in the bloodstream in this day and age. Modern science is a bitch. But it's not infallible. The autopsy will only show what they search for.

So, the best poisons are chameleons. They lurk out of sight, or masquerade as something different.

Aconite is an ancient killer. Women used to grow the pretty purple flowers in their gardens, then brew it into tea for unfaithful husbands.

I've made it into little white tablets, a quarter the size of my pinky nail. Once I drop one into Yozhin's drink, it will dissolve in seconds. He's going to swallow it down, and it's going to wreak havoc in the sodium channels of his cardiac and neural cells. It won't happen immediately, while I'm standing there. It will give me a nice little window to make myself scarce. But then, sure and certain, his heart is going to seize up tighter than a charley horse.

The coroner could find a trace of the aconite, but not without ordering a full-scale gas chromatography, which he won't do.

Not with Yozhin's blood already swimming with much more obvious culprits like alcohol and cocaine. Not to mention his sixty-some pounds of excess weight, and the fact that he's hardly a spring chicken.

Nothing could be more natural or expected than a heart attack.

The only thing I've got to watch out for is his bodyguards. There's one, a tall blond with a birthmark on the side of his face, who's already got his eye on me. Either I've done something to make him suspicious, or that's just his natural state. Either way, I don't want to tangle with anybody the size of a refrigerator.

I join the other girls out on the floor, mingling with the patrons enough that the floor manager won't give me shit, but making sure not to get pulled into any private rooms before Yozhin gets here. He should be arriving any minute.

The Raketa is a large club, glamorous in that uniquely Russian way where everything is flashy, showy, and just a little bit odd. Russians love a good theme. In Raketa, the theme is outer space. The floor and ceiling are speckled with little lights that are supposed to look like stars, and the booths somewhat resemble rocket ships. There's a giant portrait of Yuri Gagarin on the wall, watching the girls gyrate against the poles on the main stage.

I keep glancing at the clients' watches—it's almost ten o'clock, long past when Yozhin usually arrives. I'm about to give up on him for the night when I see him hurrying through the doors, looking flushed and agitated.

Yozhin is about 5'9, the same height as me, but he looks small next to his two hulking bodyguards. I can see he's brought the blond with the birthmark. Blondie is already scanning the room with a scowl on his face.

Yozhin is balding, with a short salt and pepper beard, pouchy eyes, and full lips that he licks a little too often. He wears his suits too large, probably in hopes of hiding his belly. When he tips the girls, he makes sure to slide the bills as far into our G-strings as we'll allow, with his thick little fingers lingering on our skin. We have to smile the whole time like we love it.

This isn't the first time I've posed as a stripper or a sex worker —it's an easy way to get close to my targets. Every time I do it, a little more rage builds up inside of me. I hate these men who think that their power and money buys a woman as easily as it buys a car or a watch.

I like to think of myself as a professional. I try to keep emotion out of my work. But I can't deny that I'm looking forward to seeing Yozhin's face flushing purple as his heart turns to stone inside his chest.

He deserves it. My targets always deserve it.

Yozhin's look of strain eases just a little as he catches sight of me.

"Roxie!" he cries, coming close to give me a kiss on the cheek.

"Hey, Mr. Yozhin," I say. "I was afraid you weren't going to make it tonight."

"I wouldn't miss seeing you," he says, allowing his eyes to roam freely over my body in the skimpy costume.

He pulls back from the kiss, but he lets his hand linger on my right asscheek. I'm longing to shake him off, but if I stay the course, tonight is the last time he'll touch me or anybody else.

"You want me to go get Angie?" I ask.

The sooner I get him alone in the private room, the sooner I can make my move.

"I want to," he says regretfully, "but I'm supposed to be meeting someone here tonight."

"Oh," I say, pouting out my bottom lip.

"Come sit with me though," he says. "Until my guest arrives."

I give a nod to Angie across the room. We join Yozhin at his VIP table. He buys us two of the space-themed cocktails, which are actually just pineapple juice when they're made for the strippers but cost the clients fifteen hundred rubles a round. I get a kickback every time a client buys me a drink, or any time they purchase a private dance.

Of course, those earnings pale compared to the actual payout for this job. But it amuses me to drain the bank accounts of these politicians and businessmen, who should be home with their wives instead of groping girls young enough to be their daughters.

"Where is he?" Yozhin mutters in Russian to his blond bodyguard.

"He says he'll be here in ten minutes," Blondie replies.

The other reason Yozhin likes Angie and me is because he thinks we only speak English. That's true for Angie. Not at all true for me.

My father had taught me four languages by the time I was five years old. And that was by far the least-strange thing he taught me.

I was a good student. His rules have kept me alive. One of his rules was, "What you know is just as valuable as what other people know. Never let them see what you know."

Yozhin has let all kinds of useful information pass from him to me, because he doesn't think I understand a word he's saying.

While Yozhin and Blondie are talking, Angie is stroking her fingertips lightly up and down my arm. The clients love it when the girls cuddle up together. And honestly, it feels nice. I'd rather have Angie touch me than Yozhin.

Yozhin is getting distracted, glancing over at us. He's about to reach his pudgy hand over toward Angie's bare thigh when the man he's been waiting for comes walking into the club. I can tell it's him by the way Yozhin snaps to attention, his face looking more nervous and strained than ever. It's weird to see him so jumpy.

I don't know who this guy is—he's never been in Raketa before. He doesn't look smug enough to be a politician, nor wealthy enough to be a businessman. He certainly looks mean enough to be a criminal, but he doesn't have quite the usual style of a Bratva—no tattoos or jewelry.

I just see a man in a black suit, with an extremely pale face—almost sickly-looking. There's a stiffness to his expressions, as if he's forming them intentionally, without actually experiencing the emotions he's pretending to portray.

He shakes hands with Yozhin, and his smile is the worst expression of all. It's just a straight line on his thin lips. It doesn't put Yozhin at ease any more than it does me.

Whoever this guy is, I don't want to tangle with him. I should make my exit and take care of Yozhin another night.

"Do you want to do it now?" Yozhin mutters to the man, obviously eager to get their meeting over with.

"Let's go to a private room," the man in the black suit replies.

"You can go, girls," Yozhin says in English to Angie and me.

I'm about to take him up on that. But Black Suit holds up one slim white hand to stop us, saying, "Bring them. No need to draw attention."

So, we have to follow the men into one of the private rooms, usually used for lap dances.

Once we're inside, the man in the black suit instructs us to dance with each other while he and Yozhin sit side by side on the small sofa.

Yozhin's men are stationed at the door. Black Suit's men are standing on the opposite side of the room. With Angie and me in the middle, grinding up against each other, it's difficult to watch the two men on the sofa without being noticed. Even more difficult to hear what they're saying over the pounding beat of some Nyusha song. I have to read their lips, stealing glances over Angie's shoulder.

"You know where to take it?" Black Suit is saying.

"Yes," Yozhin says hesitantly, "but this isn't what I usually—"

Black Suit cuts him off.

"Just do it. I don't want to hear any more whining."

"I don't—"

I can't see the next part because Angie has inadvertently moved in front of me, sliding her slim body up and down against mine in her bright red thong and matching bra.

I turn her around and unclasp the bra, slipping the straps down her shoulders to reveal a pair of heart-shaped pasties over her nipples. This position is convenient because I can see the men on the couch again, and it distracts the bodyguards on the opposite side of the room. They're looking at Angie's tits instead of at me.

Black Suit is passing Yozhin something small, black, flat—probably a flash drive. Yozhin takes it gingerly between his fingers before slipping it into the breast pocket of his suit.

Black Suit mutters something else, but his mouth moves so stiffly and he's bent so close to Yozhin that I can't make it out. I only see Yozhin replying, miserably, "I know. I'll be there."

But he won't make his meeting, whatever it might be. Because I'm sick of coming into this club, and I'm not dragging it out another week. Besides, I'm worried what might happen if Yozhin's deal with this guy goes south. If someone else kills Yozhin before I do, I won't get the rest of my money.

Their business concluded, Black Suit quickly finishes his drink and nods to his bodyguards. They exit the private room, leaving Yozhin alone with Angie and me, as well as the two remaining guards.

Yozhin lets out a sigh, visibly relieved to see the man in the black suit gone.

He eagerly gestures for Angie and me to join him.

"Who was that guy?" I ask, keeping my voice light. "He gives me the creeps."

"He's nobody," Yozhin says, eager to distract himself with more pleasant things. "Sorry to keep you waiting, girls."

I pretend to adjust the little triangles of leather over my breasts, slipping the white tablet out of my top.

"That's okay," Angie giggles. "We were having fun."

She's about to climb on top of Yozhin, but I grab his drink, the little white tablet sandwiched between my ring and pinky fingers. I hold the glass by its rim, so my hand hovers over the liquor inside. I release the tablet, letting it fall down into the drink, as I pass it over to Yozhin.

"Here," I say. "Business is over, time to relax."

Yozhin takes a grateful gulp of his drink, nearly draining the glass.

"You're so good to me, girls," he says, grabbing us both around the waist and pulling us tight against him.

I straddle his lap, putting my tits in his face, and letting Angie go around behind him. My body is blocking the view of the men at the door, but I can almost feel Blondie's eyes boring into my back.

As I grind my hips against Yozhin, I run my hands over his chest, feeling the slight bulge of the flash drive in his suit pocket.

I'm faced with quite the dilemma here.

I don't know what's on that drive, but I know it must be valuable.

On the one hand, it would be so easy to slip my hand inside his jacket and take it.

On the other, it's not part of my job to steal anything. I really didn't like the look of the man in the black suit. It would be stupid to tangle myself up in his business without even knowing who he is.

I really should just leave the flash drive alone.

But I'm so curious. I want to know what it is and how much I can sell it for. I'm getting tired of St. Petersburg, tired of Russia in general. The right score could set me up nicely somewhere else. Somewhere a lot warmer.

Yozhin's empty drink is sitting on the sofa next to him. I knock it off with my knee, so the glass shatters on the ground, the ice cubes skittering across the floor.

"Oops!" I say.

In the moment of distraction when the glass shatters, I sneak my hand inside his suit, and pull out the flash drive. I tuck it inside the front of my thong. There's precious little coverage there, and I'm afraid the drive will leave a lump. The blond bodyguard has sharp eyes.

I trade places with Angie, keeping my body turned away from Blondie. Angie works her hardest, grinding and gyrating against Yozhin, but he's too stressed from his meeting to focus on her. And he's beginning to feel the first effects of the aconite. I can see the flush on his skin, the increased rate of breathing.

Which means it's the perfect time for us to get away from him.

"Sorry," I say, putting on a fake sad face, "I think our time's up. Angie and I have another client waiting."

"That's okay," Yozhin says, his voice coming out tight and pinched. "I'm feeling a little off today anyway. But you girls did a good job."

He slips a few folded bills into Angie's G-string. When he tries to do the same to me, I swiftly pluck the money from his fingers so as not to risk dislodging the flash drive.

"Thanks!" I say brightly, giving him a kiss on the cheek.

Now the tricky part.

As we walk toward the door, I look Blondie straight in the face, boldly holding his gaze so he can't look down at my body.

"See you next time," I say, saucily.

He narrows his eyes at me. His lips twitch, as if he wants to say something back, but I hurry out the door before he can reply.

I make a quick detour to the change room to hide the flash drive in my boot. Then I look for a client to engage me in another lap dance.

I'm safely ensconced in a private room with two Bulgarian businessmen when I hear a muffled thud and commotion coming from Yozhin's room. I assume he's collapsed on the floor.

His bodyguards are shouting for an ambulance. The floor manager will be debating whether to risk calling paramedics into the club, or whether to hustle the minister into a private car so he can be driven to the hospital.

It won't matter which option he chooses—Yozhin will be dead before he arrives.

When I finish this dance, I'll retrieve my cellphone and send an encrypted text to my broker.

*It's done.*

## 2

# IVAN PETROV

ST. PETERSBURG

*No gangster is ever happy when he's at peace.*

— LORENZO CARCATERRA

My phone rings from the nightstand of the expensive hotel room I've booked for the afternoon. I see the name Dominik on the screen— my brother and top lieutenant. I know if he's calling me instead of texting, it must be important.

I climb off the girl I've been riding like a filly at the racetrack.

"Let them leave a message!" Nina protests, but I ignore her.

"What is it?" I say into the phone.

I hear Dominik's voice, as low and calm as ever to the average observer—only I know him well enough to detect the under-current of strain.

"We've got a problem with the shipment."

"What kind of problem?"

I can feel Nina's fingertips trying to caress my shoulder, the side of my neck, to distract me and lure me back to bed. I smack her hand away impatiently.

"Babanin got the merchandise in, but then he gave it to someone else."

"Who?"

"He won't say, but I'm guessing it went to Remizov."

"That slimy fuck," I say, furiously.

"What do you want me to do about it?"

I know whatever I tell Dominik, he'll execute it to the letter. But this was a massive shipment, and a massive betrayal by Babanin. Big enough to deserve a personal response.

"Don't do anything," I tell him. "I'm coming down myself."

"Alright," Dominik says.

"See you in ten minutes."

I hang up the phone.

"Ten minutes!" Nina says, playfully pouting at me. "That's not enough time."

But I'm already buttoning my slacks and pulling on my dress shirt.

Nina sits up, annoyed. Her dark red hair tumbles down around the full breasts her husband recently paid for but has barely been allowed to enjoy. According to Nina, he's only able to rise to the occasion about half the time anyway—the perils of marriages between young women and old men.

"Are you going to drive me home at least?" Nina asks.

"No," I say. "Get a cab."

"That's not very gentlemanly of you," she says.

"Have I ever fucked you like a gentleman?" I say, buttoning up the last button on my shirt.

Nina smirks. She thinks I'm flirting with her. But the truth is, I'm already tired of her. Why do so many beautiful women cease to be beautiful as soon as you get to know them?

Nina isn't catching on. She hops out of the bed, trying to get in front of me, running her hands over my chest and purring up at me.

"We should go on a trip together. Somewhere warm and tropical . . ."

"How are you going to explain that to your husband?"

"I'm getting tired of sneaking around," she says. "I was thinking it might be time for you and I to make things official. I was talking to a lawyer and—"

I cut her off.

"Do you think I would actually date you?"

She stops talking, her mouth hanging open and looking as stunned as if I'd slapped her across the face.

"What?"

"I said," I make my words distinct and deliberate, "do you think I would actually date you?"

"But . . . we are dating."

"No," I say. "We're fucking. There's a difference."

She's sputtering, so outraged she can't even form words.

I explain it to her, like she's a child.

"Do you think I would actually date someone disloyal enough to cheat on their husband?"

"You hypocrite!" she shrieks. "You're just as bad!"

"You spoke the vows, not me," I tell her. "You promised to honor, obey, and always be true. I never promised Egorov I wouldn't fuck his wife."

"Well you're a murderer!" she shouts at me. "You're a killer and a gangster and a thief and a . . . a . . . a liar!" she finishes, her pretty face contorted with rage, and her spit flying up in my face.

She's tearing at the front of my shirt, beating her fists against me. I grab her wrists in one hand, squeezing them with less than half my strength, but hard enough to make her squirm.

"I don't lie," I say, my voice deadly quiet. "I *always* keep my promises. So you know I mean it when I say that if you see my face again, it's the last thing you'll ever see."

She stares up at me, her eyes round with terror.

"Because you're right about one thing," I tell her. "I am a killer."

I let go of her wrists, which sink limply to her sides.

I leave her behind in the hotel room, not bothering to give her money for a cab like I usually would.

It was probably overkill, to threaten her like that. But I'm in a foul mood about the botched delivery. The idea of Nina trying to whine and cajole her way back into my life is something I don't want to deal with. Better to burn that bridge right now.

Nina Egorov is a cocktail waitress who managed to snag a low-level hustler, and now that she's tired of sucking his wrinkly old cock, she thinks she can trade up again.

Lyosha Egorov is a nobody. The fact that Nina thinks she could go from him to me is an insult.

That's what pisses me off—her thinking I was actually interested in her for more than an afternoon. Good-looking women are a dime a dozen. They literally throw themselves at me when they see a $60K watch on my wrist and the keys to a $200K car sitting next to my phone on the bar.

I wouldn't even have to be tall or handsome to get as much tail as I want, yet I'm all of those things, and powerful as well. I really could snap my fingers and have Nina killed, though I don't particularly want to.

I've never killed a woman yet. I like to think I have a few standards left.

I don't want Nina dead, but I do want her gone.

If I was going to get into a relationship—which I'm not—it wouldn't be with a woman like that.

What kind of woman would I actually date?

I have no idea.

That's why I'm single.

What kind of woman would fit in the life of a Bratva boss? An innocent flower who has no idea what I actually do? A social climber, attracted to the money and power? A mafia princess, who's at least used to this world?

I've tried them all, and none seem to suit me.

I suppose I'm just too picky. I don't even like to eat at the same restaurant twice. I can't stand anyone for more than a few hours, except my brother.

I think I'm just meant to be alone.

And I'm fine with that.

I get my car from the valet and speed off to Babanin's warehouse, where he's supposed to be storing my shipment of Kalashnikovs but has apparently given them away to somebody else instead.

It takes me almost thirty minutes to get there. Babanin's port is located on a remote rim of the Baltic Sea, far away from the city center of St. Petersburg. It's a dull and quiet little harbor. Perfect for bringing in shipments without anybody noticing. Especially when the appropriate bribes have been paid.

Dominik is waiting for me when I roll up. He's my baby brother, but we don't look much alike other than height and breadth. He's fair while I'm dark, he has a smooth, almost gentle voice, while mine can be harsh, even when I don't mean it to be.

He's the only person on this earth that I trust. Sometimes I think that without him, I'd become a complete monster. He's the only thing that holds me back from the edge. Caring about him keeps me slightly human.

"*Privetik, brat,*" he says, giving me a nod. *Hey, brother.*

"*Privet,*" I say, clapping him on the shoulder. "Where's Babanin?"

"Inside," he says.

"With how many men?"

"Two."

I consider this for a moment. I don't like to go into a contentious meeting like this outnumbered. But Babanin is an old man. That doesn't mean I discount him—but it evens the playing field a little.

"You want to call Efrem or Maks?" Dom asks, reading my mind.

I shake my head.

"No need," I say.

Dominik nods in agreement, and we enter the warehouse. I can see Babanin up in his office. He's sitting behind his desk, trying to act confident, but I know that he knows he's in deep shit.

Dominik and I climb the stairs to the office. It's a glass box, transparent on all sides so that Babanin can look down on the warehouse and the loading dock, keeping an eye on his workers at all times.

Babanin is a small man, as age-spotted and wrinkled as a tortoise. But I know he's as sharp and methodical as ever. Which is why he surprised me by giving away my guns. It's not like him to be so rash.

I go through the doorway first, Dom right behind me. Babanin has his goons stationed on either side of the door—the one on my left is a fat fuck. He looks like a sumo wrestler squeezed into a suit. The one on my right is a little more intimidating in terms of fitness, but he holds himself like a posturing peacock, not like a tactical fighter.

Without me having to give Dom so much as a look, he moves slightly to the left so that he and I are each lined up with one of the guards, in case something goes down.

But for now, my attention is on Babanin.

He's pretending to shuffle papers around on his desk. I see the nervous darting of his eyes and the slight sheen of sweat on his bald forehead. He has a bottle of gin on his desk, and a mostly empty glass in front of him.

"Ivan," he says, his voice hoarse. "You want a drink?"

"No," I say, taking a step closer to his desk.

I can feel his bodyguard shifting his position behind me, keeping close. Too close, if he knew what he was doing.

"Where are my guns?" I ask, though I already know the answer.

"My apologies," Babanin says, his hand shaking slightly as he pours another shot of gin over his melting ice. "We had the shipment come in, just as expected, but unfortunately, an unseen complication arose. But I assure you, I can get more. I just need a little time to—"

"What was the complication?"

"They were, ah, confiscated."

"You mean you gave them to someone else."

"He didn't give me any choice!" Babanin cries. "He knew exactly when they were arriving, he came in here with fifteen men, loaded them onto his truck—"

"Who?"

"Remizov."

I let out my breath slowly. It's what I expected, but I'd still hoped to hear otherwise. It's an unpleasant complication.

Remizov is the head of a new crime syndicate. They're not Bratva, not in the traditional way. Remizov doesn't represent a family, bonded by blood, shaped over generations. He's a nobody, who came from nowhere, just like his men. He doesn't follow the rules of the Bratva, spoken and unspoken.

Which is why he's taken my guns.

I have no desire to start a war with him. But he's drawn the first blood. And in my world, that has to be answered.

But first, I have to deal with Babanin.

"I find it curious that you were afraid of Remizov," I say, taking another step toward his desk. "Yet you failed to consider what my reaction would be."

"I had no choice!" Babanin protests again, holding up his hands in a gesture of innocence. "Remizov and his men were armed! And he has connections—connections in the government, at the FSB!"

"I understand," I tell him.

For a minute there's a glimmer of relief on Babanin's face. But then I continue. "You thought that our longstanding relationship would protect you. I'm afraid it's quite the opposite. It only makes your betrayal all the worse. You don't own this dock anymore, Babanin. It belongs to me now."

Babanin stares up at me, sputtering with outrage, his eyes magnified behind his glasses so that he looks more like a tortoise than ever.

"What do you mean?" he says. "That's outrageous! I've been controlling the shipments out of here since before your father was born, you . . . you . . ."

He trails off, seeing the look of fury on my face.

"You're lucky I'm letting you leave here alive," I tell him. "That's the only courtesy you'll receive from me."

Babanin stares at me in shock. He can't actually imagine getting up from that desk and not returning again. Like a tortoise, this office is his shell, his home, his protection, an integral part of himself. He thinks he can't live without it.

I see these thoughts flit across his face, and then he casts a swift glance at the bodyguard standing behind me.

I've been expecting this. The guard draws his gun from beneath his jacket and tries to point it at the back of my head. But he made a mistake when he took his position too close behind me.

I take a step backward and slightly to my left, so that his arm goes over my right shoulder, the handgun now pointed toward his boss instead of at the back of my skull.

I reach up and grab his wrist, then I yank downward and drive my shoulder upward, forcing his elbow to lock in the wrong direction. There's a sharp cracking sound as the joint strains and then snaps. The man's finger jerks on the trigger, and the gun fires directly at Babanin.

The bullet hits him in the throat, on the right side. Babanin claps his hand against the wound. There's no staunching the flow of dark blood that pours over his fingers, down onto the papers on his desk.

"Shit," I say.

I was telling the truth. I hadn't planned to kill Babanin.

Irritated with the incompetent guard, I hit him once, twice, three times in the face, until he slumps to the floor, his arm twisted at the wrong angle beneath him.

All throughout this encounter, I hear the sounds of my brother struggling with the second bodyguard. Once I've dealt with the clumsy gorilla on my side, I'm free to watch Dom as he grapples with the sumo behemoth.

The fat man is more limber than I would have given him credit for. He and Dom are wrestling and bellowing like two wildebeest. Dominik is much fitter, but the bodyguard has the advantage in mass.

My brother rears his head back and brings the crown of his skull smashing down on the bridge of the bodyguard's nose. The man goes limp, tumbling to the ground like a felled tree.

Dom stands up straight again, shaking his head to clear it and wiping the blood off his forehead with the back of his arm.

"Took you long enough," I say.

"Thanks for the help," Dom replies sourly.

"You had it covered," I tell him.

Only then does Dominik notice that Babanin is shot. He looks at the old man, pathetically slumped over on his desk.

"Did you mean to do that?" Dom says.

"I *didn't* do it. That idiot over there shot him," I say, jerking my head toward the first bodyguard.

"Well, he won't be getting his Christmas bonus," Dom says.

I look around the office, at the file cabinets stuffed full of the coded records of fifty years' worth of illegal shipments. It really is a shame that all Babanin's work came to this. But he put me in a position where I had to make an example of him or look weak in front of a rising threat.

"What do you want to do with all this?" Dom asks.

He looks equally overwhelmed by the crowded office, the fallen bodies making a mess of the carpet.

"Burn it," I tell him.

Dom takes the bottle of gin off the desk. He douses Babanin's body, the papers on the desk, the carpet and the blinds.

"What about them?" he says, jerking his head toward the bodyguards.

"Burn it all," I say.

Dom pours the gin over the bodyguards too, then pulls his lighter from his pocket. He sparks the flame and throws it down on the soaked carpet. With a soft roar, it catches fire.

We exit the office, closing the door behind us.

# 3

## SLOANE

I stay a few days more in my hotel suite, then return to my safe house in the Frunzensky District, close to the Obvodny Canal.

I had planned to work a couple weeks longer at Raketa, so there would be no connection between Yozhin dying and me quitting directly afterward. But I'm thoroughly sick of the pole dances and the leering men, and I don't want to be at the club if the man in the black suit returns to look for his flash drive.

I don't want to give him another look at my face, or another chance to get me alone in a room with him.

I always stay at a hotel during jobs, to make sure no one is tracking me. I don't want to risk anybody following me home. I know all too well that if someone can find you, they can kill you. We all have to sleep sometimes.

It's a great relief to get home to my apartment at last. As soon as I unlock the door, I can smell the familiar scents of my favorite mint tea, my Moroccan oil shampoo, and the succulent in my kitchen that can stand the neglect of a long absence.

My security system is still armed, just as I left it. I review the surveillance tapes anyway, to be sure that I didn't suffer any unwanted visitors while I was gone.

My apartment is sparse, clean, almost empty to most people's eyes. But it's exactly how I like it. Everything in it is for me alone. I never bring anyone here.

I have one chair at the table in the kitchen, one larger, overstuffed armchair in the living room. My bedroom contains a bed and a desk with a custom computer rig I built myself.

That's where I head first, to check the recordings, and then to close the file on this most recent assignment.

I already received the second half of my payment, wired immediately upon confirmation of the kill.

Now I go through my files, scrubbing all trace of Yozhin: his picture, his profile, the meticulous notes I took on his workplace, his connections, his habits. I delete it all. None of it matters now that he's dead.

Then I message Zima, my broker. He's the one who brings me all my jobs. He's my point of contact with my clients. I never speak to them directly; I never even know who they are. They talk to Zima and he talks to me.

It's a layer of protection for all of us. And it helps keep things impersonal. I don't want to know why the hits are ordered, or by whom. There can't be any judgement or emotion in my job.

My rule for Zima is that I only kill professionals. Businessmen and women, politicians, criminals. People who have inserted themselves into the jungle, into the endless struggle for power and domination. They choose to play the game, and so they deserve their fate.

I have no interest in killing some housewife whose husband is tired of her, or some old man whose family wants an inheritance.

Zima knows this, and he only sends me jobs that fit my parameters.

I like to think I've built quite the reputation for myself over the last five years. Of course, no one knows my real name. I doubt they even know I'm a woman. But they might suspect it—Zima says I've been given the nickname 'The Angel of Death'.

I don't mind it. I've been called worse.

My father's the one who taught me, trained me. At first, he was trying to protect me, in case any of the skeletons in his closet came crawling out, looking for revenge.

But after a certain point, he must have known he was creating a weapon. All those countless hours of study, of drills, of him repeating his endless lists of rules . . . what did he expect me to do with it all? Did he think I'd become a schoolteacher after all that?

"Every action, no matter how small, has a consequence."

He said that.

So, he knew what he was doing. He knew what he was making.

He made a killer.

And I'm very good at it.

I've never missed a target.

If I ever do, it will probably be my last. The one you miss is the one that kills you.

Usually, when I finish a job, I take a break. Rest and recuperate. Do some reading. Travel somewhere new.

This time I'm thinking Asia, maybe Japan. I have to get out of the snow—I can't stand a whole winter in St. Petersburg.

I send a quick message to Zima:

*Job done. Payment received. Minus your cut, of course.*

I don't expect him to respond. He's a night owl, hardly ever awake before 5:00 p.m. At first, I thought that meant he lived on the other side of the world, but after some digging, I realized he's right here in the city with me, just living some sort of vampiric schedule. No wife or kids to keep him in the land of the living.

To my surprise, I see a reply coming through almost immediately. It takes a minute to run through the decoding software, and then I read:

*I have another job for you.*

I stare at the message in surprise, then quickly type back:

*I just got home. No thanks.*

I fish in my pocket, feeling for the flash drive I stole out of Yozhin's suit pocket. I haven't had a chance to look at it yet, not having access to a proper computer at the hotel.

I pull out the drive, examining the flat black rectangle.

There's no mark on the metal casing, no indication of where it came from or what it contains.

I hear the chime of another message coming through from Zima. It says:

*You're going to want to take a look at this one. It's a big payday.*

I hesitate, twisting the flash drive between my thumb and index finger.

I don't like doing back-to-back jobs. Exhaustion makes you sloppy. And I like to let the dust settle. The closer the hits, the more likely that someone might draw connections between them. You start leaving patterns, trails of breadcrumbs for someone to follow ...

*How big?* I type.

*$500K.*

Huh. That is big. Five times my usual fee.

Which means the target is going to be a bitch to execute.

*Who is it?* I ask.

A pause, and then Zima says, *Sending the file over now.*

I wait for it to load, tapping the flash drive gently against my desk.

Because of all the layers of code Zima and I use, all the remote servers the information has to bounce back and forth between, it takes forever to download anything.

But finally, the progress bar fills and the documents begin to pop up on my screen.

Before I get a schedule or map or even a name, I see a large black and white photograph. Though it looks as if it were taken from a distance, using a telephoto lens, the man is staring directly at the camera. He's more than staring at it—he's glaring as if he wants to tear it to pieces.

His eyes are dark, set beneath thick black brows with a slight peak to their shape, giving him a permanently scowling expression. He has a long, straight, aristocratic nose and a broad jaw. His thick black hair comes almost to the collar of his suit. Unusual for a Russian, he has a slight olive cast to his skin, or at least that's how it appears in the picture—it's hard to tell since it isn't in color. The stubble along his jaw and above his upper lip straddles the line between a five o'clock shadow and an actual beard.

There's something very intimidating about this man. Confidence and power radiate from his expression, and something else . . .

Anger. Even rage.

I'm not surprised in the slightest when the rest of the file loads and I see the name and title:

Ivan Petrov, head of the Petrov Bratva.

I've killed one or two Bratva before, but never the head of a family.

And never one who looked like this.

I don't even need to read the file to know that this man will be tactically trained, experienced, well-protected.

This is a dangerous job. Nothing like slipping a pill into the drink of a pudgy politician.

I should tell Zima I'm not interested.

But $500K . . . it's half a million dollars. I could take a break after that. A very long break.

I could leave St. Petersburg for good. Set myself up somewhere sunny—Portugal, or Spain.

I never should have stayed here so long to begin with.

I stare at the picture a while longer, wondering how much nerve I've got when it comes down to it.

My father would tell me to forget it.

*Don't be stupid.*

*Don't pick a fight you can't win.*

Well, fuck my dad. He's not here to give advice anymore.

I place my fingers on the keys and type:

*I'm in.*

There's a long pause, long enough that I wonder if Zima is going to withdraw the contract. Then he types:

*Good. I'll send over the rest of the file.*

I let out a sigh. Once I have it all on my computer that's it, I'm committed.

I've got to be out of my mind to take this job.

But I've been feeling reckless lately. It was reckless to steal the flash drive, too.

While I'm waiting for Petrov's file to download, I insert the flash drive into my computer to take a look at what secrets it's holding.

It's full of several large files. My computer makes steady clicking and whirring sounds, trying to download the information. But almost at once, I see that the files are encrypted. And not in any way I recognize.

I consider myself a pretty handy little hacker. I take a poke at the files, trying to crack the encryption. After twenty or thirty minutes of trying the various tricks I know, I've gotten precisely nowhere. I have no idea what the information is and no clue how to unlock it.

It's going to take a real professional.

That's a project for another day, however.

I eject the flash drive and close it up in a little fireproof box, hiding it behind a brick in my fireplace.

Then I turn back to Ivan Petrov's file.

If I'm going to kill this guy, I need to learn absolutely every-thing about him.

# 4

## IVAN PETROV

I must admit, it gives me a pang, seeing Babanin's warehouse going up in smoke. That place had history. But if I'm going to take over the dock, better to start fresh.

The fire will send a message to Remizov. It will show him what I'm prepared to do in answer to his aggression.

That's the real problem here. Remizov is a weed that has been allowed to grow too large. When he first began taking over parts of the Zolotov and Veronin families' territories, nobody did anything about it. Those families were weak, and they deserved to lose what they had if they couldn't protect their own interests.

But then he started attacking the supply lines for the Stepanov family's heroin out of Afghanistan, and in one fateful week, he launched a bloody attack on the entire Jewish diamond district, confiscating tens of millions of dollars in raw stones, and leaving twenty bodies dead in the street, including the wife and daughters of Alter Farkas. The women had been working in Farkas' shop. They refused to give up the combination to his safe, and Remizov's men shot them dead on the spot.

It's the kind of brash and public violence that usually would have necessitated a response from the police, no matter how many payoffs had been made. But as Babanin mentioned, Remizov seems to have forged unusually strong connections with the FSB, the police, and the ministers of St. Petersburg.

The weed has spread its roots into the foundations and walls, finding the cracks and weak places. And now it's threatening to bring the whole building tumbling to the ground.

The stronger Remizov gets, the less any single family wants to attack him openly. I had no intention of doing it myself. But now he's left me no choice. His actions cannot go unanswered.

Dominik knows this too. That's why he's quiet as we drive back to the compound. He knows we're living out the last moments of calm before the storm.

I pause outside the ornate iron gates, giving Maks a salute where he's posted in the guard tower. He triggers the gates to open, and I pull the Hummer into the yard.

I live at the compound full time, with Dominik and eleven of my top lieutenants—those who aren't married or living with the mothers of their children.

It used to be a monastery. Its thick stone walls are convenient, not to mention its network of catacombs and tunnels beneath the buildings. It's also quite beautiful. That shouldn't be a consideration, but like I said, I've always appreciated history.

Most of my soldiers are related to me in one way or another—cousins, second cousins, even uncles and nephews. The Petrovs are one of the largest Bratva families in Russia—widespread and diverse. It's our strength and our weakness. I have connections everywhere in Russia and throughout Europe. But we never had a tight enough organization to be one of the major players in St. Petersburg. Until I came along.

In the ten years since my father died, I've centralized control of our businesses, our finances. What was sloppy and ineffective is now efficient and highly profitable. When there was pushback from my own family, I had to be brutal at times. I had to make examples of my own flesh and blood.

But prosperity brings fealty. I replaced those who were old and set in their ways with the younger generation. Men who are loyal to me and me alone. I've earned their respect and their trust.

My father was never able to do any of that. He cared too much what other people thought. He wanted to be liked.

The Bratva is not a democracy and never can be.

My father didn't understand that people want to be dominated. They feel safest when they have a strong leader to follow. Whether my men agree with my decisions or not, my certainty gives them comfort and motivation.

So I can never show hesitation, or fear. I have to be the leader my family needs.

Only my brother knows me well enough to see the cracks in the facade.

"I'll gather the men," Dom says quietly, once we're inside the main building.

He calls everyone into the war room, which used to be the chapel of the monastery. All the pews are gone now, the room dominated by a large, circular table, so heavy that it would probably take all thirteen of us to move it. The light filtering down from high overhead is shot through with color from the stained-glass windows depicting scenes from the Book of Revelations. The largest window shows the four horsemen of the apocalypse, riding their red, white, black, and vermillion horses. The green rider is Death himself, carrying a scythe.

Once everyone is seated, Dominik gives the men a short summary of what transpired at the docks. Then I take the floor.

"A conflict with Remizov was inevitable," I tell the men. "We may come to terms with him in time, but that can only be done from a position of strength. So, his affront must be answered."

I nod my head to Efrem on my right side—a burly cousin of mine, who's as dark and hairy as a Siberian bear, but much more intelligent than he looks.

"Efrem. Find out where our guns were taken and make a plan to get them back."

He gives a curt nod. He's my second lieutenant, after Dom. I know I can trust him to find the missing shipment.

I turn to Maks, who is as blond as Dom, and looks almost frail, but happens to be one of the most vicious fighters I've ever known. He nearly decapitated his stepfather with a broken bottle when he was only thirteen years old.

"Find out who's protecting Remizov in police and government positions. Figure out why there was no response to the diamond district massacre."

Farkas was well-connected and well-respected. I can't imagine what kind of pull Remizov must have obtained to allow him to so recklessly slaughter Farkas' wife and daughters.

I turn to one of my youngest soldiers: Karol. He's only nineteen and he looks it. He's already become popular in the compound because of his good nature and work ethic. I know he's got friends all over the city, and as one of our newer members, he won't necessarily be known to Remizov or his men.

"I want you to follow Remizov," I tell Karol. "Don't get too close. But send me a record of his habits and movements, and anything that might be useful to us—any mistresses, or interests, or dirty little secrets. I want to know where he shops, where he eats, where he gets his hair cut, who he visits, who he fucks. Send it all to me."

"You got it, boss," Karol says with a grin.

"And maybe tone down the shoes," I tell him. "They're not exactly stealthy."

Karol looks down at his trainers, which are bright orange and probably cost some obscene amount of money, despite how extraordinarily ugly they are.

"Right," he says, trying to force his face into seriousness. "Good idea, boss."

Now I turn to Dominik.

"Once we get our guns back," I tell him, "we need to make a strike of our own. Remizov hits us, we hit back twice as hard. Find the target."

Dom slowly nods without speaking. His blue eyes are clear and serious.

The rest of the soldiers are full of energy and excitement. They like making plans. They like taking action. To them, this is almost like a rugby match. Our team has been attacked, and they relish the idea of mounting their own offensive in return.

Dom isn't thinking about pride and glory. He's thinking about what the worst-case consequences might be. He's thoughtful by nature. In another life, he might have been a philosopher instead of a gangster.

But he was born into this family, with me as his brother. So he'll follow me down this path, no matter what might be at the end of it.

"I'll find a target," he promises me.

I nod and clap him on the shoulder.

While my men are busy, I'll start meeting with the heads of the other houses. I'll shore up my alliances, and perhaps build bridges where none have been before. I'm not the only one who knows Remizov is a threat.

# 5

## SLOANE

*The supreme art of war is to subdue the enemy without fighting.*

— Sun Tzu

The more I study Ivan Petrov, the more I realize I might have made a terrible mistake in taking this job. He's going to be extremely difficult to hit. He lives inside a veritable fortress—an old monastery outfitted with every possible piece of modern security. He's constantly surrounded by his soldiers, particularly his younger brother, who is just as tall and stacked with muscle as Ivan himself.

There aren't many female assassins for a reason. Despite what movies and TV shows would have you believe, there's almost no way that a woman can win a fistfight against a man of above-average height and strength. When some ninety-pound actress takes out a beefcake stuntman with one punch, I can only roll my eyes.

My success has always been a result of stealth and the element of surprise. I'm no hero—I take my targets while they're sick, while they're sleeping. I poison them, suffocate them, or snipe them from a distance.

I try never to get close enough that it comes down to a fight, because there's a good chance I'd lose, even with the endless hours of training I received from my father. That's the unfortunate reality of being 5'9 and 135 lbs.

To kill Ivan Petrov, I'll probably have to get a lot closer than I'd like. He doesn't follow a regular schedule or routine. He's unusually watchful. And he travels around in an armored Hummer that's basically a tank.

Plus, he's jumpier than usual because, apparently, he's in conflict with some other Bratva boss. Details are thin on the ground, but I've watched him visiting the heads of various families, plotting alliances for whatever's about to go down.

I don't know anything about Bratva rivalries, but I wonder if Petrov's nemesis is the person who hired me. It would be the quickest way to end the conflict before it even starts.

The Bratva usually dole out violence personally—they're not afraid to get their hands dirty. So they're not my typical clients or targets. But I don't think Petrov's rival is a typical Bratva.

The way people talk about him, he sounds more like a boogeyman.

If he is the one who hired me, it's all the more reason why I can't drop this job, much as I might like to. I don't want the boogeyman after me.

And I couldn't back out of it anyway—it would destroy my reputation. Once you have the full file, you have to carry out the hit. Or risk having a contract put out on your own head.

I've got to do the job, and I've got to do it soon.

The more I try to follow Petrov around, the more likely I am to be spotted. It's already become clear to me that the only place he goes regularly is his compound. That's where I'll have to take him. Which means I need to figure out a way to break inside.

My first tactic with a break-in is to find the firm that did the security system and steal the schematics. However, it appears that Petrov did the work himself, or had his men do it. I can't find a record with any of the usual firms, or even any permits filed with the city.

However, scouting the compound, I can see some of the systems I'll have to bypass: two guards stationed around the perimeter at all times. Cameras mounted all around. Twelve-foot-high medieval-era stone walls. Dogs patrolling the grounds.

The dogs scare me more than anything. A dozen Caucasian Ovcharkas—Russian prison dogs. Big, heavy beasts that are fearless, intelligent, and ruthless. Their brindled coats protect them from knives or blows or the coldest winter winds. Six of them can take down a full-grown bear. They'll rip me to shreds if they get a scent of me.

It's the problem of these dogs that gives me my entry point. I've been wracking my brain all week, trying to think how I can get inside the compound without them smelling me.

I have to drop down on the roof, or tunnel underground.

And that's when I realize, the tunneling may already have been done, four hundred years ago. While I haven't found any maps of the monastery online, that doesn't mean that they don't exist.

So I visit the archives of St. Isaac's Cathedral. There I find a map so faint that I have to sneak a photograph of it, then enhance the faint brown lines on my computer, extrapolating the areas that have been completely eradicated by friction and crumbling paper.

There are tunnels beneath Petrov's monastery.

And one of them begins outside the walls. It might be caved in or bricked up—generations have passed since this map was made. But I won't know until I try.

I gather my gear and ready myself to break into Ivan Petrov's house.

THE ENTRANCE to the tunnel is down an old well, on the backside of Petrov's property. It takes me nearly an hour just to find the well, which has lost so many stones that it rises only a few inches off the ground and has been boarded over as well. With the thick leaves on the ground, and several inches of dirty snow, I might never have found it at all if I hadn't happened to step directly on it, hearing the hollow sound of my foot striking the rotted wood.

I pull up the covering and peer down into the black hole of the well.

I'm not entirely certain how a well can also be an entrance, but this is an exploratory mission. I don't expect to get all the way to Petrov tonight—though I'm ready if I do.

Strapping myself into a rappelling rig, I wait until I'm fully inside the well to turn on my headlamp. This well is only a few hundred yards from Petrov's walls, and I can't risk his guards spotting my light.

I expect it to be cold inside the well, but it's actually warmer than it was above ground. There's no wind down here. The thick earth and stone all around me provide insulation.

It smells like wet dirt, worms, and decay.

When I look down, I see my headlamp reflecting on black water far, far below me. If my rope breaks, I'll be trapped like a bug in a test tube. Assuming I survive the fall.

No point in thinking about that. I try to focus on the walls instead. If there really is some kind of door, it must be above the waterline, or else the tunnel would flood.

It's hard to tell stone from the dirt in the dim light, especially with the tangles of roots that have burst through the walls of the well. It gives the shaft an unpleasant, animalistic feel. As if I'm descending into the throat of a beast.

I almost miss the door, until my headlamp glints off the ancient iron handle. I grip the metal ring and try to pull the door open. It's so intractable that I think it must be locked. I tear away the creeping roots to see if I can find a keyhole. I'm quite good at picking locks.

I see only the iron ring, however. So I try to pull it once more, bracing my feet against the slippery stone walls on either side. With a shrieking groan, the door inches open.

I climb into the tunnel, unhooking my harness.

I had thought the well was dark, but it still received a little starlight from the sky above. The tunnel has the true blackness of the heart of the earth. Without my headlamp, I wouldn't be able to see my hand two inches in front of my face.

The tunnel is narrow. I can't stand upright. I have to walk along slowly, hunched over. Any moment I might come to a pile of rocks, or a brick wall, or a steel security door.

My hope is that Petrov doesn't know about this tunnel, wherever it comes out within his compound. I saw on the map that it ended in what used to be a cellar, but of course I don't know if that room exists now, or to what use Petrov might have put the space.

It's difficult to judge how far I've come. I'm losing sense of time and space, with the darkness and my slow, hunched over gait,

Unexpectedly, the tunnel comes to a fork. Two paths branch off to the right and the left.

That's not what my map shows. One of these routes must have been dug later. I have no idea which way to go.

The tunnel hasn't run straight thus far—there have been several long, winding changes in direction. I don't know where I stand in relation to the compound.

So all I can do is guess.

I go left.

I walk and walk for what feels like forever. The tunnel seems to stretch on interminably. Surely I should have come to the end by now?

I'm starting to get claustrophobic and paranoid. What if the tunnel branches again and again? What if there's a labyrinth under here, and I'm lost and wandering for days, not able to even find my way back to the well?

And what if when I get back, someone has found my rope and cut it?

I can feel my heart rate rising, my skin starting to sweat. The tunnel feels hot, as if it's going deeper and deeper into the earth.

I touch the walls.

It's not my imagination—they really are warm.

I look up and see a wooden hatch in the roof of the tunnel. I push up on it.

This is the most dangerous part so far.

I have no idea where I'm coming up. I might be entering the middle of the dining hall, with a dozen men all around me. I've come at night when they should be asleep, but I'm dealing with a houseful of bachelors—I doubt they're all tucked in bed by midnight.

I can hear noise, a sort of hollow, clanging sound. A groaning and rushing. There's a dim red light as I crack the hatch.

Once the hatch is up, I have to jump up to get my arms out so I can pull myself up. It's hotter than ever, and the banging noise is very close.

I peek out and find myself in the boiler room, right behind an extremely large and ancient copper water heater. The hatch can only open partway, because it's wedged between the heater and the furnace. That's why it's so hot and noisy.

I have to squeeze out, trying not to burn myself against the copper.

I ease the hatch closed behind me, watching the lid nearly disappear into the patterned grain of the floorboards. The hatch has no handle or lever to pull it up again—I won't be able to get it up quickly if I have to escape this way when the job's done.

Still, I feel a sense of calm now that I'm actually inside the monastery. My heart rate slows. My breathing steadies.

It's as if my body goes into a kind of hibernating state, allowing me to be perfectly quiet and still. As I slip through the monastery, I will have to be as silent as a shadow, as unobtrusive as a piece of furniture. I pull my stocking down over my face and sneak out of the boiler room.

It must be 3:00 a.m. by now—the quietest hour of the night.

The stone hallways of the monastery are deserted and only dimly lit. The compound has electric lights of course, but they're set in rustic wooden sconces. In fact, all the decor seems to be old-fashioned in nature. I see several side tables, mirrors, and tapestries that I'm sure are antique.

I'm surprised by the elegance of this place. I expected a gaudy gangster's palace. Whoever chose these pieces has taste, refinement. They appreciate the history of the building.

In the silence of night, I might almost believe I've gone back in time to the era of the Orthodox monks. But, of course, if I encounter someone, it will be a Bratva brother, not a man of god.

I have to find Ivan Petrov's room. Since he's the boss, I assume he has the largest and most private quarters. I have an idea they're in the west wing of the compound. The few times I watched Petrov entering the main building, he seemed to turn in that direction before the doors closed behind him.

I move slowly, ever so slowly through the main building. I slip from one hiding place to the next. From a set of velvet drapes, to a pillar, to a stone statue in its niche.

As I draw close to what seems to be the dining hall, I hear low voices inside. I'll have to pass by the open doorway to continue on my way. I wait, hearing at least two men in conversation. When they start chuckling at some joke, I hurry past the doorway, resisting the urge to glance inside.

In my relief, I almost run into another soldier patrolling the hallway. I have to dart blindly into the nearest room to avoid him, without checking to see if anyone is inside. It's a billiards room, with an impressive bar along the far wall. Mercifully, it's empty, except for a young man snoring on the sofa.

He looks like a teenager, his caramel-colored hair long and shaggy, and his feet, propped up on the arm of the sofa, encased in bright orange Spalwarts. He's got a bag of chips spilled on the floor next to him and his phone resting on his chest. It looks like he fell asleep mid-text.

I don't like seeing someone that young here. I'm only thirty-one, but he looks like a kid to me.

Well, it shouldn't surprise me. The Russian mafia is a family business, after all. They're raised in it.

Not that different from my own situation, I suppose.

I was only six years old the first time I fired a gun. Eight when my father forced me to hold my breath again and again in a bathtub full of ice water. Twelve when he made me survive three nights alone in northern Maine in the winter.

I know my father wasn't right in the head. The problem is that when you work for the CIA most of your adult life, it's hard to distinguish between paranoia and actual threats.

It took me longer than it should have to figure out something was wrong. That some of the things my father was seeing weren't actually there. The cars "following" us. The "messages" he was being sent.

I had no frame of reference. I'd never attended a normal school. I had no friends. My father was my whole world. He was the smartest, most capable person I knew. The idea that he might be crazy was just . . . too horrible to accept.

I push those memories to the back of my mind. I can't get distracted.

I've cleared the ground floor of the west wing. If Ivan Petrov's rooms are on this side of the house, they must be upstairs.

I climb the stairs, entering a hallway that seems to lead to several bedrooms. All the closed doors are identical. Which one is Ivan's?

As I keep walking, there's a break between the doors, with a library on the left, and what looks like an office on the right. And then beyond that, at the end of the hallway, a set of double doors.

Bingo.

If there's a master suite beyond those doors, it surely belongs to Ivan Petrov.

Does he lock his doors at night?

I carefully test the old-fashioned handles. They move easily beneath my hand.

With aching slowness, I crack the right-hand door.

It's dark inside the suite, the blinds drawn. I slip through the door, closing it silently behind me. I stand still, letting my eyes adjust to the gloom.

I believe I'm in a sitting room, with the bedroom somewhere beyond.

Holding my own breath, I think I can hear the slow inhale and exhale of someone sleeping close by. It's the breathing of a large man, broad in the chest. Large lungs, a vast, slumbering body.

Ivan Petrov. I know it.

I've watched him from a distance. I've seen his intensity, his ferocity. The way his men snap to attention when he comes close, the way they obey his orders without question. I've seen his vigilance, the look of intelligence on his face. And, of course, I've seen his massive, powerful body. He wears a suit every day, but I've seen the round muscles of his shoulders and biceps even beneath the thick material of the suit jacket.

I don't want to get in a scuffle with this man. Nor do I want to risk firing a gun in a house stuffed full of his soldiers, not even with a silencer and a pillow wrapped round it.

So I've brewed up a special cocktail for Ivan Petrov. I take it out of my pocket now.

A single syringe of clear amber fluid. Once I drive it into his neck, he'll be immobilized in moments. It will flood through his bloodstream, turning his limbs to stone. His chest will seize up until he won't be able to draw a single breath. Remembering his mass, I've used enough paralytic to freeze a race-horse in its tracks.

It won't look like an accident, but that wasn't a requirement of the job. I just have to kill him and get out without getting caught.

I move through the sitting room, into the bedroom beyond. With the minute amount of light coming through the cracks in the blinds, I can just barely see Ivan's vast form, laying on the bed. He's sprawled out on his back, one thick arm flung up over his head. His heavily muscled and tattooed chest is bare. There's a patch of dark hair in the center of his chest, and a thin line trailing down the center of his stomach, disappearing under the sheet.

I suspect he's completely naked under there, without even a pair of boxer shorts. I can't help glancing toward the bulge under the thin sheet. It's a shame to kill a specimen like this, right in his prime.

But there's half a million dollars on the line. And if I don't kill Ivan Petrov, someone else will.

So I might as well get my money.

I approach the bed. Nothing could be more silent than my feet, taking step after step across the thick oriental rug. I wear the same kind of shoes that rock-climbers wear—thin, flexible, grippy. Little more than leather slippers, and quiet as bare feet.

Petrov's head is thrown back on the pillow, his throat exposed. His dark hair tumbles across his eyes. His lips are slightly parted. His breathing hasn't changed—it's still a steady metronome. But I'm about to put a stop to it.

I slip the cap off the needle. I grip the syringe in my fist, my thumb above the depressor.

As I raise my right hand in the air, above his neck, I can't help glancing one more time at Ivan's face.

His dark brown eyes are open, staring up at me.

# 6

## IVAN PETROV

I wake as soon as my door opens.

I've always been a light sleeper.

The slightest change in light in the room, the smallest sound will wake me.

I know it isn't one of my men. They never come in my rooms, not ever. If something happens, they just call my phone, which is charging on the nightstand right next to me.

I don't know how many intruders there might be, or if they're armed. If they're wearing night-vision goggles, they'll be able to riddle me with bullets before I can even roll off the bed.

So I force myself to stay perfectly still. I keep my breathing calm and steady, though my heart is racing.

I wait, listening to the near-imperceptible sounds of someone approaching the bed.

Just one person. Incredibly quiet and light on their feet.

How did they get into the compound?

The alarm never went off. There were no sounds of a struggle —that would have woken me up way before the door opening.

I feel a flush of fury, the closer they get.

How dare this intruder come in my house? Into my bedroom?

It's outrageous.

But I'm also the smallest bit impressed. Nobody's gotten this close to me before.

I can feel the figure approaching, more than I actually hear them. I feel the movement of air across my bare skin as they near the edge of my bed. I hear the rustle of their clothes as they take something out of a pocket.

I try to look at this person through a slit in my closed eyelids.

It's dark in the room, and the figure is dressed all in black, like a shadow come to life. I can see that they're only average height, and slim.

Now I'm just waiting to see if they've got a knife or a gun.

I have a Glock under my pillow, and another in my night-stand. An AR under the bed and more weapons in my closet. But as the figure raises its hand, I can see I won't need any of that.

They're only armed with a syringe.

The needle tip glistens in the starlight coming through the blinds.

It looks wickedly sharp.

It sends a flush of pure rage through my veins.

This fucking coward planned to sneak in my room in the middle of the night and jam that needle in my neck while I was sleeping.

The assassin raises the syringe over my throat.

I open my eyes and look up into their face.

I see two wide, startled eyes looking back at me. In shock, the assassin hesitates.

That's all I need.

I launch myself off the bed, grabbing their wrist in my left hand, and driving my right shoulder into their body.

The would-be hitman is ridiculously light. He goes flying backward, crashing down onto the floor with my full weight on top of him. He's still trying to twist the syringe, to jam it into the back of my hand, so I wrench it out of his fingers and fling it across the room.

I'm tempted to stab it into his chest instead—give him a literal taste of his own medicine. But I don't want to fuck around with that needle of death. For all I know, the slightest prick could kill me, and it's too easy to get scratched in a fight.

I intend to throttle this little shit instead. However, he's not easy to hold onto. He's wriggling and thrashing beneath me. Now that he's lost his weapon, he's obviously abandoned any hope of winning the fight. He just wants to get away.

He's so slim and light that I'm sure he's lightning fast. I have no intention of letting go of him. But he's fighting like a wildcat, kicking and punching and squirming, trying to snatch up anything he can get his hands on.

He grasps the bedside lamp by its cord, yanks it close enough to grab hold of the base, and tries to bring it crashing down on my skull.

I knock it away with my arm, then swing a haymaker at his head that he only just manages to dodge, my fist brushing past his nose.

He responds with a kick to my groin. It just misses the mark, his heel striking my inner thigh instead. It still hurts like a bitch and makes me double over. I'm going to have a bruise the size of a softball.

Enough fucking around.

I seize the assassin by the throat. I'm going to squeeze the life out of him.

But I want to watch the light fade from his eyes as I do it. So I grab the stocking covering his face and I tear it off his head.

And I'm face to face with the most beautiful woman I've ever seen.

I stare at her in utter shock.

She stares back at me, my body pinning her down, our faces inches apart.

She's flushed with color, panting hard from our fight. I can feel her body quivering beneath mine, her heart pounding away against my chest, as rapid as a rabbit's. She's trapped. Like a wild animal, she's desperate to flee.

I can't understand how I didn't realize her gender when we were rolling around on the floor. I suppose it's because I never could have imagined a woman breaking into my room to kill me.

I'm mesmerized, staring at this face that's flushed with exertion and sheer terror.

Her dark, almond-shaped eyes are wide and bright, thickly lashed and framed by straight black brows. She has a heart-shaped face with a slightly square chin, offset by a remarkably wide, full-lipped mouth. Pulling off the stocking has loosed a halo of black curls all around her cheeks and shoulders.

I can't tell who she is or where she's from. With those dark eyes and hair, and that lightly tanned skin, she could be French, Iranian, Greek, Albanian . . . I only know she's not Russian. Because I've never seen anybody who looked like this before.

It takes me a moment to remember that she was trying to murder me.

And I'm supposed to be paying her back in kind.

Yet somehow, I find my fingers loosening around her throat.

I don't let go of her—I'm not that stupid.

But I find myself in a conundrum.

I've never actually killed a woman before.

I'm not against it, in principal. After all, this is the very definition of self-defense. Whatever she had in that syringe, I know for damn sure it wasn't a vitamin B-12 shot.

She would have jammed it into my neck without hesitation.

I should do the same to her now.

But I just can't.

Part of it is the sheer destructiveness of the act. This woman is absurdly gorgeous. And she's obviously smart too—she managed to sneak past all my security, all the way into my bedroom without getting caught. Killing her would be such a waste. Like smashing the Venus de Milo with a sledgehammer.

There's another reason I don't want to kill her: she's made me curious. Who is she? Why did she come here?

For practical reasons alone, I should find out who sent her.

So I let go of her. But as I do so, I say, "If you move one millimeter, I'll snap your neck. Don't test me."

I see a shiver run down her body. But she doesn't let her fear show on her face. She watches me, expressionless.

Without taking my eyes off her, I pull my kit bag out from under the bed. I take out a couple of zip ties, and I say, "Lay down on the ground, with your hands behind your back."

For a moment, she hesitates. I see her eyes dart toward the window, the door.

She must know she won't get far, not with me awake and not dead, and a whole houseful of soldiers ready to be summoned with a yell.

Slowly, she lays down on the carpet, her face turned to the side, and her arms behind her back.

I zip tie her wrists, a little tighter than necessary, because I'm limping from her kick to my groin. Then I tie her ankles for good measure.

I pause, looking down on her.

I need one question answered. The answer is going to determine her fate, at least in the next five minutes.

"Did you hurt any of my men on the way in?" I ask her.

"No," she says.

Her voice is low and clear. It doesn't sound like she's lying.

"That's very lucky for you," I tell her.

I leave her lying on the floor and go to the next room over to wake up my brother.

# 7

## SLOANE

I'm in deep shit.

When you work a job like mine, you know that someday you'll probably meet a bad end. You just hope it will be quick—a bullet to the back of the head that you don't see coming. A slash from a knife that bleeds you out in moments.

What you don't want is to be captured by the Bratva.

Because once you're captured, you're at their mercy.

And the Bratva don't have any mercy.

My father knew a thing or two about interrogation techniques. It's part of the standard CIA training.

He used to tell me, "It's impossible to withstand torture. Any decent torturer, given enough time, will break you. All you can do is resist interrogation by preparing yourself for the methods they'll use to manipulate you."

My father was tall, with sandy-colored hair and blue eyes. In pictures of his younger years, he looked a bit like Steve McQueen. But by the time of that conversation, he'd grown thin and haggard, his hair too long and his face half-hidden by his dark blond beard. He wore tactical clothes almost all the time, so he could keep knives, firearms on his person, even when we were at the grocery store.

"Tell me how they'll try to get you," he said, his frantic eyes boring into mine.

I was thirteen years old. Skinny, needing braces, but moving cities too often to see an orthodontist regularly.

I listed off the techniques, counting them off on my fingers. "Sleep deprivation. Torture. Mind-altering substances. Diet manipulation. Sensory deprivation."

My father nodded, his head jerking with each one.

"And the psychological techniques?"

"Suggestibility. Deception. Humiliation. Pride and ego. False friendship."

While we spoke, I was trembling slightly. Because we were down in the basement of the house we were renting, and behind my father I could see a bench. A cloth. And three gallon-jugs of water.

"You can't withstand it," my father kept repeating. "All you can do is resist as long as possible, until your information is no longer useful."

He'd made me practice withstanding pain before.

But I knew that waterboarding was nothing like holding my hand in a bucket of ice water.

As he became more and more agitated, I kept looking over his shoulder. I was so scared of those jugs of water. I was so scared of what I knew was coming next.

Even though it humiliated me, even though I knew it might only make him angrier, I started to cry.

That time, and that time alone, my tears seemed to snap him out of his manic state. He looked at me. He seemed to actually see me for once—a frightened teenager, snot-nosed and red-eyed. His face softened.

"It's alright, Sloane," he said, putting his arm around my shoulders. "That's enough for today."

The next time we went down to the basement, the jugs of water were gone.

Now I'm down in the basement again. But not at my father's house. I'm in the catacombs of Ivan Petrov's compound. He carried me down himself, slinging me over his shoulder like a sack of potatoes. Then he set me down on a chair in the middle of this tiny room, my wrists bound behind me and my ankles tied together.

He used several more zip ties to secure my arms to the backrest of the chair and my feet to the legs. Then he disappeared upstairs, leaving me alone in this small, barren room, lit by a single lightbulb dangling from the ceiling.

Other than the chair I'm sitting on, there's one other equally uncomfortable wooden chair, a stripped mattress in the corner, a sink, a toilet, and four blank walls. The floor is made of hard-packed dirt, and the walls look like plastered stone.

There's a camera in the far corner of the room, nestled up against the ceiling. I'm tempted to make a face at it, but I resist.

Fear always brings out the most obnoxious side of me.

Rudeness is my coping mechanism.

It's not a very good coping mechanism.

As soon as I'm alone, I try twisting my wrists and hands, seeing if there's the slightest slack that might allow me to slip my hands free. But this isn't the first time Petrov's used a zip tie. I'm trussed up like a Thanksgiving turkey and I'm not getting free.

The anticipation is awful. I try not to let myself imagine what's going to happen when Petrov returns. My father always said this was the most effective thing of all: letting the captive wait. Letting them drive themselves mad with fear.

But it doesn't matter if I understand the techniques Petrov might use, or if I can prepare myself for the pain of torture.

Because the problem is, I don't have the information he wants.

I already know what he's going to ask me.

He wants to know who hired me to kill him.

I honestly don't know the answer.

That's why the contract comes through a broker: so the client doesn't know me, and I don't know them. It protects the client, so I can't spill their secrets. And it protects me, so they're not tempted to cover their tracks by getting rid of me once the job is done.

That's the way it works.

But Ivan Petrov isn't going to believe that.

I don't know which alternative is worse: him believing me, or him thinking I know nothing.

Because the only thing keeping me alive right now is his curiosity.

It's hard to tell how much time is passing. There are no windows in this room, and I can hardly hear anything from above, except the odd bump or creak, which might be a chair moving or someone walking around, or just the bones of this ancient building shifting in the wind.

As impossible as it might seem, with the peril and physical discomfort of my current situation, I'm starting to get sleepy. That's the effects of the adrenaline wearing off. I've been in a state of high anticipation for hours now. My body can't sustain it. I'm just plain tired.

The ancient wooden door creaking open snaps me to attention.

It's Ivan Petrov.

He's back. And he's alone.

He stands in the doorway, the harsh overhead light turning his face to a mask of sharp lines and shadow. His dark eyes are boring into me, drilling right down into my soul. It takes everything I have to hold his gaze, to keep my face steady and still.

No matter what happens, I'm determined that I'm not going to break down like I did when I was thirteen years old. I won't blubber and cry.

Ivan Petrov approaches slowly. I can hear the heavy sound of each footstep. He's put on a white dress shirt, the sleeves rolled up to expose his thick forearms with their covering of dark hair. He's wearing slacks and polished black loafers. He's combed his dark hair back from his face. Probably showered as well—his hair looks slightly damp.

He takes hold of the empty chair, then drags it closer to me. He sits down so that we're facing one another.

He leans forward, his elbows on his knees, and his hands loosely clasped in front of him, knuckles facing upward. His change in posture sends waves of movement across the slabs of muscle on his shoulders and arms, beneath the thin material of the dress shirt. His hands are huge, the knuckles slightly misshapen. From pounding, hitting, breaking bone.

I'm all too aware how strong this man is. Up in his bedroom, he overpowered me in moments. It was like trying to wrestle a lion—he and I aren't even the same species. I didn't stand a chance against him then, and I certainly don't now, tied up and locked in this tiny room with him.

He's silent, staring at me.

That means the interrogation has already begun.

As my father always said, "He who speaks first loses."

So I keep my mouth shut, as the tension stretches out between us.

At last, Petrov says, "Why did you come here tonight?"

He has an extremely deep voice, with a harsh edge to it. Anger simmering right below the surface.

I can tell he's just as keyed up as I am. I have no intention of playing games.

"I came here to kill you," I reply.

His right eyebrow quirks upward. He's surprised I admitted it so readily.

"Why?" he says.

"I was hired to do it. That's my job—it's nothing personal."

"It's a little personal to me," Petrov says.

There isn't a hint of a smile on his face, but I hear the amusement in his answer all the same. This man is a brute, but he has a sense of humor.

"How did you get in?" he asks me.

I consider if I should answer.

If I do manage to escape this room, the tunnel would be my best route out of the compound. If I tell Petrov about it, he's sure to close it off.

However, I don't have a good lie prepared. If I tell him I scaled the walls, he'll check the security tapes and see that's not true.

"There's a tunnel into your compound, from a well out in the woods," I tell him. "I can show it to you, if you like."

I want him to untie me and take me out of this room.

But Petrov isn't fooled that easily. He stays sitting exactly where he is.

"Maybe later," he says.

He reaches into his pocket and pulls out my syringe. He doesn't have the cap for it (that's still in my pocket), so he's put a piece of cork over the tip. The transparent, amber-colored fluid is pretty enough, but it has a sinister gleam to it. Like snake venom.

"What's in here?" he says.

"My own little cocktail. Mostly paralytics."

"Not very sporting of you," he says.

That edge of fury is back in his voice. I need to choose my words carefully.

"Well," I say, "as you saw, I'm not much of a brawler."

"You know how to fight though," Petrov says, tilting his head to examine me. "Where did you learn that?"

He's genuinely curious. I can tell he didn't plan to ask that question, but he wants to know the answer.

I need to walk a fine line here. Giving a captor personal information can be a good way to gain their trust. Still, I don't want to tell Petrov too much. I'm holding onto a shred of hope of escaping this mess. If I get away, I don't want him tracking me down afterward.

So I say, "I learned from my father. He was in the military."

"Here?"

"No. In America."

"You're American?" he asks, surprised again.

"Yes,"

"What are you doing in Russia?"

I'm not telling him that. I just shrug.

"I've lived a lot of places."

Petrov folds his arms across his broad chest, the syringe still clutched in one large fist. He's looking me up and down, trying to figure me out. I can see his thoughts whirring by behind those deep brown eyes. He's intrigued, and that's good. Intrigued is better than enraged, or worse of all, bored.

"What's your name?" he says.

"Sloane."

"Sloane what?"

"Ketterling," I reply, giving him my mother's maiden name.

I see a flicker across his face.

Dammit. He can tell when I'm being evasive.

"Well, here's the thing, Sloane," he says, his voice low and soft. But not gentle—the very opposite of gentle. "I know that you're aware of the predicament you've gotten yourself into. You tried to kill me. I think I'd be justified in returning the favor."

Can't argue with that.

"But we're both professionals," he says.

That's an appeal to common ground. Someone trained Petrov in interrogation techniques as well, or he's just a natural.

"I don't want to have to resort to threats of violence."

I think he just did.

"Instead, why don't you just tell me what I want to know?"

"You want to know who hired me to kill you," I say.

He nods, his eyes drilling into me. "That's right, Sloane."

"I would love to tell you," I say. "But I don't know the answer."

A flush of anger across his face—this is a man who does not like being opposed.

"It's true," I insist. "That's how the contract works. It goes through a broker. I don't know who hired me—I never do."

"Who's the broker?" Petrov demands.

"I don't know that either."

That's only partially true—I know a few things about Zima. I know he lives in the city. I could probably figure out where. But I don't want Petrov tracking him down either.

Petrov senses the partial deceit. His fist clenches tighter than ever around the syringe.

I'm concerned that he's going to use that as his instrument of persuasion. If he sticks me with even a tiny fraction of the liquid within, he won't get a chance to ask me any more questions.

But Petrov tucks the syringe back in his pocket and reaches behind him for something else.

A knife, pulled from the waistband of his dress slacks.

It's a DV-1, a combat knife from the Far East region of Spetsnaz. I have one very similar, back home at my apartment. It has an absorbent leather handle and a matte black carbon blade. But the distinctive part of this knife is the small, semi-circular indentation on the base of the blade. It allows you to rest your finger there, to get a better grip, as you pull the knife out of the body of your enemy.

Petrov stands up from his chair. He seems to be moving in slow motion as he approaches. He points the tip of the knife at me. He positions the blade at the base of my stomach.

Then he slices upward, in one swift, sure motion, cutting through the material of my shirt.

He slits the fabric from base to neck, and then with two quick slashes he cuts down the sleeves as well, pulling the whole top away.

Though he's moving deliberately fast, showing me how easily he could cut me to ribbons, the same as he did to my shirt, he hasn't left a single scratch on my body. I feel the cold metal whisper across my skin, but there's no pain.

Crouching down, he pulls my shoes off my feet, and my socks. Then he slices away my pants.

Now I'm tied to the chair in only a sports bra and panties. He hesitates a moment, then he cuts the bra away too, the knife flashing upward between my breasts.

He takes a step backward, his eyes roving hungrily over my body. With my arms bound behind my back, my breasts are thrust upward for his perusal. I can feel my nipples stiffening from the chilly air, and from the heat of his gaze.

No matter how hard I try, I can't meet his eyes now. I'm looking down at the floor, unable to hide the bizarre mix of emotions racing through me.

I'm embarrassed, yes.

Afraid, of course.

But also, inexplicably, horribly aroused.

It's sheer madness. But I can't help it.

I've spent years learning to suppress my emotions, to keep control of myself. I can't be careless in my line of work, or impulsive. I can't succumb to fear.

So, these days, it takes a lot to get a rise out of me.

Being tied naked to this chair, with this brutal, virile man looming over me . . . that's doing it. That's breaking down the barriers fast.

I have to get a hold of myself.

I look up at Ivan Petrov, forcing myself to meet his eye once more.

In my most saucy tone I say, "Well, that's only fair. After all, I already saw you naked."

I see a tug at the corner of his mouth, a sharp exhalation of breath that might almost be a snort of laughter.

I see the slightest tremble of his hand. Not the one holding the knife, the other one. I think he wants to reach out that hand to touch me . . .

But he stops himself. He scoops up my shoes, socks, the remnants of my clothes. He carries them out of the room and locks the door behind him.

I'm sure he's going to search the pockets of my clothing, but he won't find anything useful. It's not like I carry around a driver's license and a Rolodex.

For now, I'm left alone in the cell once more. It's a lot chillier without my clothes. But somehow, my skin is still burning.

# 8

# IVAN

G oddamn that girl.

I'm back up in my room, pacing the floor.

What the fuck am I doing?

I should just kill her and be done with it.

Either she really doesn't know who hired her and she's of no use to me, or she does know but she's determined not to tell me. In which case, I'm going to have to get it out of her, using methods that turn my stomach just to think about.

In the end, the result will be the same—I have to kill her. Because what's the alternative, just let her go?

She'd probably turn around and put a bullet in my head the next day. She's a hitman! A hitwoman. I don't know what the fuck you even call it, when it's a girl so goddamned gorgeous that you can hardly look at her without throwing her down on the floor and fucking her.

I hear a soft knock on my door.

I know it must be my brother.

I don't want to let him in right now—I'm too agitated. But I stride across the room and throw the door open, seeing Dominik's expression of concern.

"Did you find out who put out the hit?" he says.

I clench my fists, not wanting to admit it to him.

"No," I say through gritted teeth.

"Do you . . . want me to assign one of the other men to do it?"

"No!" I bark at him. "No one goes down there but me."

The idea of any of my men even entering the room where Sloane is tied to that chair fills me with a fury that I can't understand.

All I know is that she belongs to me, and me alone.

She's my prisoner.

"Well, it's obviously Remizov who hired her, don't you think?" Dom asks me.

"That seems most likely," I agree.

I have plenty of enemies, but there's only one person I've started a war with in the last twenty-four hours.

"Do you want to put out a hit on him in return?" Dom asks.

"That's not how we work," I say sharply. "If I want Remizov dead, I'll kill him myself."

"Alright," Dominik says, holding up his hands.

I don't know why I'm biting his head off. He hasn't done anything wrong.

"He doesn't know we've got his assassin," I say. "He might even think I'm dead. So, here's what we do: I'll lay low. Let him think he's been successful. You get our guns back. Then we hit back. We crush this little bastard once and for all."

Dom nods. He turns as if he's about to leave but hesitates a moment in the doorway.

"What about the girl?" he says.

"I said I'll deal with her," I snap at him.

He nods and leaves.

I will deal with Sloane.

But I have no idea how.

Dom knows that Sloane tried to kill me.

And Maks saw me carrying her down to the catacombs, which means that everyone else in the house is going to know about it by lunchtime.

She has to be punished, if only to maintain my standing in the eyes of my men. They can never perceive me as weak, or uncertain.

And the truth is, I want to punish her . . .

But not in the way my men would expect.

This girl has confused me, infuriated me, and tied me up in knots.

I want to take out that frustration on her.

I want to break her like I'd break a wild horse.

By dominating her. Taming her. Training her.

I look at my watch.

It's 7:20 a.m. I can hear some of my men starting to stir around the house. But most will sleep until nine, or ten, or even noon. Most of our work is done in the evening or during the night.

Sloane hasn't slept at all yet.

As I shift my weight, I feel the throbbing ache on my inner thigh where she kicked me.

I should leave her tied to that chair until her fucking arms fall off.

I won't, though.

I leave my room, taking a spare blanket out of the closet on my way down the hall. I descend the stairs, past the dining hall, over to the doorway to the lower levels. It's a hidden doorway that looks identical to the other wooden panels of the wall.

The monks had their secrets. The lower level is riddled with passageways and hidden rooms, and below that, the catacombs themselves, which once housed the tombs of the dead brothers. My men dug them all out, altering the space to suit our purposes.

I was aware of two tunnels leading out of the monastery—I keep them open in case we ever need to pass in or out of the compound unseen. But those tunnels have locked steel doors and surveillance. I don't think that's how Sloane got in.

Which means there's a third tunnel that I didn't know about.

That annoys me. It's sloppy.

Sloane will tell me where that third tunnel is, and how she found it. She'll tell me everything I want to know, whether she wants to or not.

I've reached the door to her cell. I check the camera outside to make sure she hadn't somehow slipped her bonds and is now waiting next to the door to try to brain me with the chair.

She's still tied up. And still distractingly nude.

I straighten my shoulders, trying to steel my resolve.

I have to maintain control.

This girl isn't some mafia princess or gold digger or club rat. She's a professional, like me. She's going to do whatever she can to get under my skin.

As I push open the door, she looks up at me. Her arms are still pinned behind her back. She must be getting extremely uncomfortable by now, but she's refusing to show any hint of that.

I can't help allowing my eyes to sweep down her body once more.

Fucking hell, what a body it is.

I've seen a lot of beautiful women naked.

But there's something about her figure that arouses me like nothing ever has before.

Perhaps it's those bare breasts, thrust toward me—small and natural, but beautifully teardrop-shaped, with the most delicate, tender-looking nipples. Maybe it's her long limbs, slim but lightly muscled. Maybe it's her thick, black curls and the slight tint of color in her skin that adds to the mysterious look of her, the ambiguity of who she is and where she came from.

Or maybe it's just the fact that, tied to that chair, she's so deliciously vulnerable.

I've dominated women in bed, but never quite like this.

The sight of her bound and helpless is achingly erotic. It's awakening something inside of me I've never known before.

It's waking a beast.

And that beast is hungry.

She sees the lust in my eyes. Her lips part ever so slightly. Her breath quickens.

I try to make my voice as cold and stern as possible.

"I'm going to cut those ties," I tell her. "If you try to attack me, or to escape, I'm going to wrap you up like a mummy. So don't do anything stupid."

I see her look of surprise that I would cut her loose. Then her glance toward the door. She can't help herself, thinking how she might escape.

"It's locked," I tell her flatly. "There's a camera up there." I point to it. "And there's a dozen men between you and any door out of here."

"I know," she says calmly. "I'm completely trapped."

She's acting like she's resigned to that idea, but she doesn't fool me. I know she'll be out of here like a rabbit the moment she gets a chance.

She'll learn soon enough.

I go around behind her and slice the zip ties holding her to the chair.

She lets out a sigh of relief, massaging the red marks on her wrists.

I loose her ankles too, taking a step back in case she gets any bright ideas.

She just stands up, bending and stretching a little to get the blood flowing once more.

Her breasts sway as she leans first to the left, then the right.

I see the lines of her hipbones above the skimpy waistband of her panties, and the round curve of her ass as she turns to stretch.

I'm astonished that I ever mistook her for a man, even in her tactical gear. There's never been a more luscious, feminine figure.

I can feel my cock swelling inside my boxer shorts. It presses painfully against the fly of my trousers.

I hold the folded blanket in front of me to conceal it.

"Did you bring me some clothes?" she asks, looking pointedly at the bundle of material.

"You can earn your clothes back," I tell her. "Food and water, too. But you need to answer my questions. And not your half-truths, either. I know when you're lying."

"Then you should know that I have no idea who hired me," she says angrily, tossing her dark curls over her shoulder. The movement makes her bare breasts bounce and sway once more. Goddamnit, this is so much harder than I expected.

I won't let her distract me. I glare down into her face, standing closer than is really safe, daring her to try to hit me again.

"I want the name of your broker," I tell her.

"I don't know it."

But there's that flutter of her thick, black lashes. The slightest suggestion of a blink. It's her tell, when she's not being entirely honest.

"You know something about him," I growl at her.

"How do you even know it's a him?" she says, raising those straight black brows. "You really need to reexamine that gender bias."

I step even closer to her.

"*You* need to rethink your strategy," I tell her. "No one knows you're here. No one cares. Why are you protecting this person? He's not coming to save you. You want to draw this out, but for what? I'm the one with all the time in the world. You're the one who's going to get colder and hungrier by the day."

I throw the blanket at her so she stumbles backward a little as she catches it.

"I'll give you some time to think about it," I tell her.

Then I leave the cell, locking the door behind me once more.

This girl is intelligent. She's used to doing whatever she wants, when she wants. I don't have to torture her—the boredom of captivity will do it for me. Every hour that passes is going to torment her.

I leave her alone for a few hours to sleep.

But I'm already planning our next encounter.

# 9

# SLOANE

*Pummeling an answer out of someone never works.*

— PAMELA MEYER

I wake to the sound of the cell door opening once more.

It's extremely disorienting being in this windowless room without a clock or a watch. I have no idea if I've been sleeping one hour or ten.

I sit up, stiff from the threadbare mattress. I have a fantastic bed at home in my apartment. It's my biggest luxury: a thick down comforter, expensive sheets, a cooling pillow . . .

There are a lot of things I'm already starting to miss, being stuck in this cell.

Ivan comes through the door once more, carrying a bowl of something that smells delicious, like cinnamon and nutmeg. Of course, I haven't eaten in a while, so I'm far from picky. Almost anything would smell good right now.

The earthenware bowl is held in his left hand. In his right, he's carrying a black leather bag, something like a doctor's kit. I don't like the look of that nearly as much.

I consider standing, but then I'd have to choose between draping the blanket over me like a toga and being naked once more. Both seem like embarrassing options. So I remain seated on the mattress, the blanket wrapped around my shoulders.

"Did you get a good sleep?" Ivan asks.

He keeps his face stern, but I can tell there are hidden reserves of humor under that harsh exterior. He's aware of the ridiculousness of his question. He knows he's goading me into a saucy answer.

"I prefer memory-foam to straw and canvas," I tell him. "But I'll still give you three stars in my Airbnb review."

That twitch of his lips again. I'll get him to smile eventually.

He sits down on the ground across from me, heedless of whether the dirt floor might mark his slacks. He sets the leather bag on his right side, and puts the bowl down on his left, just out of my reach.

He sees me eyeing the food.

"Hungry?" he says.

"A little," I reply, lifting my chin.

"Our chef made this. Slow-cooker oatmeal, with cinnamon and heavy cream."

He picks up the bowl, holding it between us but not offering it to me yet.

I notice there's no spoon.

He scoops up a dollop of the oatmeal on his index and middle fingers. He holds it out to me.

I stare at him, confused.

"Go ahead," he says.

He wants me to lick it off his fingers.

I know what he's trying to do. Taking my clothes. Making me eat out of his hand like a dog.

He's trying to break me down. Trying to humiliate me.

I could refuse to eat.

But I really am hungry.

The stress of the previous hours has drained my body. The rich, delicious scent of the food drifts up to my nostrils.

Ivan is right that he has all the time in the world, while I'm only going to get more and more miserable.

I open my mouth slightly and lean forward.

I close my lips around his fingers, taking the food.

"Good girl," Ivan says, his voice low and approving.

That voice sends a thrill running down my spine.

He's smiling. Pleased with me.

The oatmeal really does taste phenomenal. As soon as it hits my tongue, my stomach clenches and gurgles, demanding more.

Ivan can hear it.

He scoops up a little more and holds it out to me.

God, this really is embarrassing. And strangely intimate. I've never let a man feed me before.

I can't stand being put in a subservient position. I need to take back the power. Exert myself on him, as he's trying to exert himself on me.

So when I lean forward to take the next bite, I look up into his eyes. I open my lips and slightly extend my tongue. As I take the food out of his hand, I let my tongue trail along the under-side of his fingers. And I suck ever so gently on his fingertips.

I see the flush of color rising up his neck, from beneath the crisp white collar of his dress shirt.

He's not the only one who can play games.

He's not the only one who can offer temptations.

As he holds out the next bite, he lets his thumb trail over my lips. I lick his fingers clean, and his hand touches my cheek. His fingers trail down my throat, down to my collarbone and the swell of my breasts beneath the blanket thrown round my shoulders.

But then he stops.

He sets the bowl to the side.

"I know you're a wild thing, *malen'kaya lisa*," he says. *My little fox.* "But what you'll come to understand is that I'm going to tame you."

A shiver runs over my skin.

I've never submitted to a man before, and I don't intend to submit to this one. No matter how intimidating he might be.

He bends over his leather bag and unzips the top. I can't see what's inside. I'm not sure I want to know.

He takes out a coil of rope—soft, black, neatly wrapped. He unfurls it, his eyes fixed on mine.

"Here's how this is going to work," he says to me. "I'm going to ask you questions. If you answer honestly and fully, you'll be rewarded. If you lie to me, or you try to be evasive, I will punish you."

Oh Jesus.

My heart flutters against my ribs.

He loops the rope around my wrists with two quick twists and pulls my arms over my head. He lifts me to a standing position, then threads the rope through a hook hanging from the ceiling. The roof of the cell is low, and he's so extremely tall that he can reach the hook without even stretching.

But I'm pulled up on my tiptoes, my arms overhead, and my body completely vulnerable. My heart is racing. I'm terrified, but there's much more than fear causing the adrenaline to flood through my veins . . . there's also anticipation.

It's insane. I can't believe what I'm feeling.

I want him to touch me.

I want him to take me.

He takes a blindfold from his bag and covers my eyes, plunging me into darkness. I feel more vulnerable than ever. Instantly my sensations are heightened. I can feel the slightest breeze across my bare skin. I'm hyper-aware of the heavy tread of his footsteps circling me.

He's prowling around me, deliberately disorienting me.

He's close, but not quite touching me.

Not yet.

"First question," he says, in that rough, deep voice. "Where's the tunnel that let you into my house?"

I bite my bottom lip, trying to decide whether I should tell him or not. I wanted to keep my escape route clear. But unfortunately, now that he knows the passageway exists, it's only a matter of time until he finds it. Trying to keep the information to myself is hopeless.

"It starts in a well, on the north side of the property, just outside the walls," I tell him. "It comes out in your boiler room."

"Good," Ivan says. His voice is like the tongue of a beast lapping at my skin—rough and soft at the same time.

I feel his huge hand caressing my left breast. His palm cups the bottom of my breast, and his thumb slides across the nipple.

I can't help but let out a groan of pleasure. Oh my god, I can't even control myself for five seconds. At his very first touch I'm moaning like a whore.

I tell myself that I won't make another sound. I'll pretend not to like it, no matter what he does.

But his hand is sliding down the curve of my side, down to my hip, and then across my navel, below the bellybutton. And now he's slipping his fingers inside my panties, all the way down to my pussy lips. I'm already breaking the promise I made, I'm already letting out little gasps and moans of encouragement as he rubs his fingers back and forth across my clit, moistened with my own wetness.

All too soon, he pulls his hand away. I can't see anything, but I have the sneaking suspicion that he's put his fingers to his lips, to taste me.

Nothing has ever prepared me for this.

If this is his interrogation, he's going to have my social security number in five minutes.

"You like that, little *lisa,*" he says. It's not a question. He knows that I love it. "See," he says, "It's better to be friends than enemies, don't you think?"

I'm ready to be his best friend if he'll keep touching me like that.

"Next question," he says. "Who's your broker?"

Uh oh.

I really don't know the answer to that.

I have a little information about him, but nothing I want to share with Ivan.

"I told you, I don't know," I tell him, trying to make my tone as sincere as possible.

"You did tell me that," Ivan says. "But I'm afraid I don't quite believe you."

I can hear him moving off to my right. I hear the distinct sound of objects shifting about as he rummages around in his leather bag.

My heart rate, already on par with a fast jog, speeds up to an absolute sprint.

He's coming around behind me.

I hear the whistle of air, and then a sharp CRACK as he swings something toward me. I hear the sound, and then I feel the sting of a leather crop coming down hard on my ass.

"Ouch!" I yell, trying to twist around.

Another CRACK! He's smacked the other asscheek even harder.

"I told you I don't know his name!" I protest.

"But you know something," Ivan says.

CRACK! He's whipped me again, in the same spot as the first time. Goddamnit, it's really starting to sting.

CRACK! Back to the left side again.

I can only imagine the welts this is leaving on my nice, smooth bottom.

CRACK!

CRACK!

The sound is almost worse than the pain. It makes me jump every time.

And this goddamned blindfold—I can't anticipate where he's standing, which side he's going to hit. I seem to feel each blow ten times as acutely with my eyes closed.

CRACK!

CRACK!

CRACK!

He's not even breathing hard. I'm all too aware of Ivan's strength and stamina. He could probably whip me like this all day long.

"I have his IP address!" I blurt out. "I know he lives in the Tsentralny District."

Ivan stops whipping me with the crop.

"You see, my little fox. I always get what I want in the end. So you might as well give it to me to begin with."

He's reaching back into his bag. I think he's going to punish me again, but it turns out to be quite the opposite.

I hear a buzzing sound. Then I feel a vibrating wand pressed against my clit, through the material of my panties.

Oh my god. If I was squirming around before, it's nothing to how I'm twisting and writhing now. Even through the thin cotton, the sensation is almost unbearably intense. The vibrator sends waves of pleasure across my belly, down my legs, until they tremble beneath me, and I'm hanging from my wrists, the rope the only thing keeping me upright.

But then, just as I'm about to explode into orgasm, Ivan pulls the vibrator away.

I give a groan of frustration and outrage.

"Not so fast," Ivan growls. He's standing so close that I can feel the heat radiating off his skin. I can feel his breath on my bare shoulder.

"Tell me why you came to St. Petersburg," he says.

Goddamn it.

There's no reason not to tell him the truth.

Except that I don't want to.

This cuts to the heart of my most vulnerable and personal information. Something very painful to me. My greatest weakness exposed.

But he'll know if I lie.

He'll know if I keep my secret.

My lips are trembling. So is my voice.

"I came here looking for my father," I tell him. "He used to work for the CIA. He said they were calling him back here for one last job."

I hear Ivan take a step backward. He's surprised. That's not what he expected me to say.

"Did you find him?" he asks.

I let out my breath in a long sigh.

"Yes," I admit. "I found him."

"Where was he?"

"In a morgue, on Nevsky Prospekt."

"Was he killed by the FSB?"

I let out a short laugh.

"No," I say. "He was hit by a taxi in Decembrists Square. Nobody called him back here. He was just wandering around, out of his mind."

I can feel Ivan's hesitation.

It wasn't the answer he expected to get.

But a promise is a promise.

I hear the buzz as he switches the vibrator on once more.

He pulls my body tight against his, one thick, strong arm wrapped around my back, the other pressing the vibrator tight against my clit.

"Let it all go, little *lisa*," he whispers in my ear.

And I do let go.

I erupt, into a climax beyond anything I've felt before. I bite down hard on Ivan's shoulder, through the crisp white dress shirt. It stifles my scream as I cum again and again against his hand.

## 10

# IVAN

I tuck Sloane back into bed, drained and exhausted.

I leave her alone in her cell and practically run back up to my own suite, to strip off my clothes and stand under a pounding hot shower spray.

My cock is so hard it feels like it's about to split its skin.

I soap up my hand and give three quick strokes before I explode, filling my hand with boiling hot cum.

My mind is full of the image of Sloane's naked body, shaking and quivering under my touch. Her vulnerability, with her arms above her head and the blindfold across her eyes. The way her full lips parted to let out each moan . . .

And the sound of my riding crop coming down on her full, round ass. The way the flesh bounced, and the bright line of red striped that flawless, silky skin . . .

I don't know what I enjoyed more: her pain or her pleasure.

It's only the beginning of the depraved things I want to do to her.

My lust for this woman is so extreme, so overpowering, I can't keep hold of it. I had to leave, before I lost control completely.

It's strange. I've never left a woman without getting my own satisfaction. This is the first time in my life where a girl's climax was more interesting to me than my own.

Watching the waves of pleasure rolling through Sloane's body was more erotic than anything I've ever felt myself.

But that doesn't mean I don't want to unleash myself on her.

Quite the contrary.

Unfortunately, I have other business to attend to first.

Sloane has been occupying my mind since the moment she broke into my room. But I can't forget that she's only the weapon pointed at me by a much bigger threat.

Wherever Remizov is right now, he's not allowing himself to be distracted by some girl. He's focusing on me and my complete and utter destruction.

I get out of the shower, toweling myself off and pulling on a fresh set of clothes.

It's 8:00 at night. I need a status report from my men.

I call Efrem, who's on his way back from tracking down the guns. I tell him to hurry back, then I go down to the main level to wait for him in the war room.

While I'm waiting, I check my messages.

I see that Karol has been texting me. He's been following Remizov from the diamond district to a restaurant on Avenue Liniya. His last message was at 5:20 p.m.:

*I followed Remizov to the Abajour Cafe. He's eating quiche and salad. Which is kind of a bitch meal. Maybe that's his weakness—he likes girl food. We could lure him with chocolates and Cosmopolitans.*

I can't help letting out a snort. I should be harder on Karol— he's reckless and hubristic, as all young people are. It's hard to always be the heavy, though.

All my relationships are with subordinates. Even my own brother has to take orders. I don't have anyone who's an equal to me.

I laugh and joke with my men. Eat meals with them, box with them, watch movies with them.

But at the end of the day, I'm the boss.

It can be lonely.

I'll have a talk with Karol when he gets back. Make sure he's taking his work seriously, not taking any unnecessary risks.

For now, I simply text:

*Where are you now?*

I wait a moment, but I don't see the three dots indicating that he's about to respond.

Efrem comes into the war room, brushing the melting snow out of his hair. It must be coming down again—I haven't even looked outside.

Dominik is with him. He looks tense and jumpy.

"We found the guns," Efrem says at once. "They're at a warehouse in Primorsky."

"Good," I say. "Let's go get them back."

"Alright," Efrem says, but I can see the hesitation on his face. He glances over at Dominik.

"What is it?" I say.

"There were only two guards on the warehouse," Dom says.

"So?"

"I dunno. Seems . . . a little too easy."

"What, you want them at the center of a labyrinth, guarded by a Minotaur?"

"Remizov isn't stupid," Dom says. "He took the guns for a reason."

"Because they're worth two million dollars," I say.

Dom nods. But he's not convinced. And neither am I, even while I'm saying it.

I've been looking at Remizov as a thug, because he's brutal in his methods, and he doesn't follow the code of the Bratva—the very few rules that even our kind abide by.

However, that doesn't mean he's an idiot. He's been extremely strategic in analyzing and attacking the weakest members of the underworld in St. Petersburg, slowly expanding his power without ever triggering a full-scale war with the more powerful families.

Until now.

He's taken a shot at me, because he thinks the Petrovs are assailable. He thinks I'm arrogant. He thinks I'll underestimate him.

Which I have been doing, so far.

"Alright," I say to Efrem and Dom. "We won't get them back tonight. We'll watch and wait another day."

"Sure," Dom says, as if he's just following my orders. But I can see the relief in his face.

My phone vibrates in my pocket.

I see it's Oleg, calling from the front gate.

"What is it?" I ask.

"A car pulled up," he says. "We approached, but it just dropped off a package and sped away back down the road."

"What kind of package?"

"Just a box. Two feet tall, maybe."

"Don't touch it. I'll bring the dogs."

I hang up the phone.

The dogs are trained to sniff for explosives or drugs. Though I doubt anybody dropped off a nice little care package of cocaine for me.

I go out to the kennels and get Volya, my favorite. He whines eagerly when he sees me. He's a good dog; he loves to work. I raised him from a puppy, along with three of his brothers.

He runs to my side when I call him. He's dancing beside me, wanting to thrust his nose into my hand, but knowing not to do it until I reach out for him. I give him a quick scratch behind the ears as a reward for his restraint.

He trots along beside me as I walk toward the entry posts, Dom following after us. Oleg and Maks have already opened the gates. They're standing out in the snow, waiting for me.

The bright halogen perimeter lights illuminate the drive. The thick white flakes of snow seem to hang suspended in the glare.

I can see the plain cardboard box, sitting out in the middle of the road. It's not even taped shut, the top flaps tucked in on each other to keep it closed.

"*Zapakh,*" I order the dog.

Volya clears his nostrils with five or six quick snorts. He approaches the box, sniffing along its top and sides for the chemical vapors of TNT, water gel, RDX, urea nitrate, or hydrogen peroxide. The most likely components of the most common types of bombs.

If he scents any of the chemicals he's been trained to search for, he won't touch the box. He'll just sit down sharp—the signal that he found something.

However, Volya does not sit down. Instead, he begins to whine in a plaintive, high-pitched tone. I call Volya my big baby. He's more intelligent than his brothers, but he's not as vicious. He's a little more nervous, and eager to please.

But I've never heard him make that sound before.

I nod at Maks.

"Check it out," I say.

Maks walks forward, his hair a halo of white blond under the light. I see his hand trail unconsciously to the gun at his waist, as if he might want to shoot whatever's in the box.

He lifts the flap. Then he stumbles backward, cursing.

Without thinking, I've already strode over to join him.

"Boss—" Maks says, but I'm already looking inside.

I see Karol's head staring up at me. Eyes open. Face horribly bruised and beaten.

My stomach rolls so hard that I can barely swallow back the vomit. I am immediately aflame with bright, burning, unquenchable rage.

Dom is standing next to me. He's seen it, too.

"Ivan," he says, laying a restraining arm on my shoulder.

I shake him off.

"Gather the men," I say, through gritted teeth. "We're going to kill that motherfucker."

I expect Remizov to have gone to ground—I expect him to be hiding like a rat in a sewer, after having sent that provocation to my fucking doorstep.

But my men haven't even finished suiting up and bringing the cars around, before Efrem tells me that Remizov isn't hiding at all. One of our informants says that he's sitting in the Lux club right now, cool as can be, having a drink.

I'm shaking with rage. I want to firebomb the club, turn it into Vesuvius with Remizov inside.

But there's probably two hundred innocent people in there.

Even in my absolute fury, I don't relish the idea of murdering waitresses and bartenders and clubgoers along with Remizov and his men.

They are his unwitting human shields. But that won't stop me from marching in there and dragging him out by his greasy black hair.

We drive to the club in three cars. I post Jasha, Oleg, Maks, and Efrem outside, so Remizov can't slip out the back. Jasha and Oleg point their guns at the bouncers, to prevent them from warning anyone inside. Dom, Andrei, and Vadim follow me inside.

I have my Glock in my hand. I plan to walk up to Remizov and put a bullet between his eyes. I know he'll have his own men inside, but if it comes to a shoot-out, so be it. I'll put my men up against his any day.

The club is dark and throbbing with loud, repetitive music. It aggravates the rage-fueled headache beating inside my skull. The air is thick with smoke and the scent of spilled drinks. I head straight for the VIP booths at the back of the club.

I see Remizov sitting there, bold as brass. His pale eyes glitter as he looks up at me, watching me approach. His face is stiff and sickly white, like a wax mask. His thin mouth is twisted up in a smile that doesn't crease any other part of his face.

My finger tightens against the trigger of the gun. I'm about to raise the barrel, to point it at his face.

But then I see the other men in the booth, seated on either side of Remizov.

Krupin, the Minister of the Kalininsky District.

Utkin, the Commissioner of Police.

And Drozdov, the Governor of St. Petersburg.

I stop in my tracks. I know I must look supremely stupid, standing there with my mouth hanging open.

Remizov's smile widens.

"Ivan Petrov," he says. "Why don't you join us?"

There's an empty chair pulled up to the table, directly across from Remizov.

Almost as if it was put there just for me.

Remizov must have assumed that his assassin was unsuccessful when Sloane failed to check in after she tried to kill me.

So he killed Karol instead.

He sent his head to my doorstep.

And then he sat here waiting for me to arrive. Timing it to the minute, I'm sure.

He's manipulating me like a pawn on a chessboard.

And like a trapped chess piece, I can only move forward one square.

I sit down in the chair, my gun resting on my lap, pointed at Remizov's stomach from beneath the table.

I'm so angry that my hands are shaking, my jaw rigid. My men are standing behind me, ready to open fire at my command. But I know they recognize the minister, the commissioner, and the governor. They know as well as I do the almighty shit storm that would reign down upon us if we start shooting.

Remizov has human shields alright, but it's not the waitresses and college students I anticipated. It's the three most powerful men in the city.

Remizov fixes me with his cold, pale eyes.

"I was just speaking with the governor about the terrible rise in crime rates St. Petersburg has been experiencing," Remizov says. "The conflicts in Moskovsky. The shootings in the diamond district. The fire at the docks."

Of course, Remizov is responsible for all of those things, including, to my mind, the fire at the docks—which I set, but only after he stole my guns.

"It's not good for tourism in St. Petersburg," the governor says, looking sternly in my direction.

"Moscow is starting to take notice," the commissioner says.

"The Bratva are becoming unruly," Remizov says, his voice soft and sibilant. "I think we're all in agreement that it's high time that the families of the city come under centralized control."

"Under whose control?" I laugh. "Yours?"

"That's right," Remizov says, unembarrassed.

My finger is itching to pull the trigger, to blast a hole in his guts right where he sits, smug and smiling.

But I know these men aren't sitting at the table with him simply to enjoy the expensive drinks. Remizov has made some kind of deal with them. He's paid them, or else he has leverage. Or both.

If I kill Remizov, I'll bring down the wrath of the men who run St. Petersburg. I'll lose more of my Bratva. I might not make it out of here myself.

My brother is right—I've sorely underestimated Remizov.

"This is the only time I'll extend the olive branch to you, Petrov," Remizov says. "I suggest you accept my offer."

"Was Karol's head an olive branch?" I say through gritted teeth.

There's a lot of things I might have forgiven, for practical reasons. But I will never forgive that.

"You're out of your mind if you think the generations old Bratva families are going to submit to some thug with no house, no name, no history," I tell him.

I can see the minister shifting uncomfortably in his seat on my left-hand side. He's from an old Bratva family himself, on his mother's side.

"The Stepanovs and the Veronins have already agreed to my terms," Remizov says calmly.

I can't hide the look of shock on my face. For a moment I think he must be lying. But there's no faking his smugness, his satisfaction.

"Then they're even bigger fools than I thought," I say.

I grab the Mamont sitting next to me and take a swig directly from the bottle. The liquor burns my throat but helps steady my hand.

I look Remizov dead in the eye.

"There will be no peace, no agreement between us," I tell him. "You're going to pay for what you did today."

On my right-hand side, the commissioner says warningly, "Petrov, you ought to—"

I hold up my hand to cut him off.

I look around at the other men.

"Remizov's honor is worth nothing. His deals with you are worth even less."

I can see the minister looking uncomfortable once more. The other men stare at me, stone faced. They've made their decision. They've aligned themselves with Remizov, which means they're my enemies now too.

Especially the commissioner. Our relationship has always been tenuous at best. He's glowering at me with an expression that tells me clearly that what little courtesy the police offered to my business, to my men, is now at an end.

I stand up.

I'm loathe to leave like this, with Remizov in a position of dominance at the head of this table. With me slipping my gun back inside my jacket, having failed to avenge Karol.

But in this moment, what else can I do?

I can only swear to myself that the next time we meet, I will kill that loathsome cockroach.

# 11

## SLOANE

When I wake in Ivan's dungeon once more, I'm feeling refreshed and ready to get into trouble. I have to say, I rather enjoyed my interrogation. But that doesn't mean I'm content to hang around here forever.

The first thing I do is examine the lock on the door and the hinges. It's an electromagnetic lock, with an armature plate. It appears to be fail-safe, which means that it would automatically unlock if the power failed. But of course, I have no access to the power supply from in here.

There's also no way to pick the lock, even if Ivan hadn't taken all my clothes, with their hidden caches of tools.

My next point of examination is the camera up in the corner on the left-hand side of the door. I grab my mattress, dragging it over to that corner and flipping it on its side so I can climb up on top of it and take a closer look.

It's a fairly standard cam, wired so it can be viewed remotely. Ivan might be watching me right now from his phone. I could disconnect the feed, so he's blind to the interior of the cell. Then I could try to attack him on his way in. But he's not sloppy enough to come strolling in blind.

I open up the back of the camera to see if there's some way to loop the feed, but once again I need some goddamned tools and probably a laptop too.

I'm pretty tricky, but I'm not MacGyver—I need more than a Bobby pin and a stick of gum. Not that I have either of those things anyway.

I take a look at the toilet and the sink—if I could rip either of those out of the wall, it's possible that the plumbing has a wide enough gauge that I could get out that way. Unlikely, but possible.

However, both are made of steel and are firmly bolted in place.

I drag the mattress back where it belongs and sit down to scheme some more.

I have a lot of ideas of ways to get Ivan to let me out of the room. But when he finally returns, when he unlocks the door and stands there looking at me, all my plots go flying out of my head. Because I see that his face looks furious, frustrated, and something else . . .

Can it be . . . sorrowful?

Something terrible has happened.

His eyes look darker than ever, wild and haunted. He's lost that look of confidence and composure.

Stranger still is the reaction this causes inside of me.

I actually feel sorry for him.

I tried to kill this man. He captured me, held me prisoner.

Then he gave me the strangest and most intense sexual experience of my life.

And now he's making me feel something else altogether—compassion. An emotion I almost never indulge, especially not when it comes to criminals, gangsters, targets.

What's happening to me?

We're staring at each other with this insane tension between us. I don't know what he's come down for, what he wants.

But I know what I want.

In four steps I've crossed the room, and so has he.

We meet in the middle.

He snatches me up in his arms and I put my hands on either side of his face, pulling him down to me.

Our mouths crash together in a kiss that is hungry, desperate, full of need and desire. My lips part. His tongue comes in to find mine. I can taste him, rich and warm and distinct. His rough stubble scratches my face. His massive hands are gripping my flesh, his fingers digging into me.

I'm tearing at his clothes, ripping open his finely-tailored white dress shirt. I hear the sound of buttons popping off and rolling away across the floor. All I care about is the sight of his thick, broad chest exposed to my view once more.

My very first sight of Ivan was in the nude, but I was hardly in a position to appreciate it at the time. Now I can feast my eyes on his smooth, deeply tanned flesh: the sheets of muscle rolling tightly under his skin, the sharp cuts on either side of his abdomen, pointing down to exactly where I want to go . . .

I fumble with the button of his trousers, then yank down the zipper. I slip my hand inside and free his cock, stiff and throbbing against my palm.

I've been with enough men to know that the size and appearance of their package rarely correlates with their skill in bed. However, every now and then, you meet with a cock that's so beautiful that just the sight of it is arousing.

That's what I find now, in Ivan Petrov's pants.

His cock is thick, smooth, perfectly proportioned. The same lovely, uniform brown as his skin, and nicely groomed. It looks so good that I do something that I almost never do.

I drop down to my knees and take him in my mouth.

His skin slides silky smooth across my tongue. His cock tastes almost as good as his lips—with the same rich, slightly salty flavor. I fill my mouth with him, my lips bobbing up and down his shaft, while I squeeze the base of his cock with my hand.

Ivan lets out a long, satisfied groan. He thrusts his hands into my hair and holds my head but allows me to dictate the pace and depth of my movement.

I run my hands up and down his thick, muscular thighs while I continue to suck his cock. I can feel him rocking his hips as the waves of pleasure start to build. I'm bringing him closer and closer to climax, my tongue dancing across the head of his cock, lapping at the ridge where the head meets the shaft, then running down the length of it once more.

His legs are trembling. He's pulling my hair without even meaning to.

I'm willing to take him all the way, but he stops me. He wants much more than that.

With a roar of lust, he scoops me up off the ground and throws me down on the mattress in the corner. He tears off my panties, literally tears them into pieces as if they're made of paper.

But even in his eagerness, I discover that he's quite the egalitarian. He positions himself between my thighs to return the favor.

He licks and laps at me so aggressively with his soft, warm mouth and the rough stubble of his chin, that it's almost more than I can take. I squirm and wiggle, but he grabs my hips and holds me tight, attacking my pussy with his mouth and even thrusting his tongue inside of me.

I start to cum. That only makes him lick harder and faster. I grip his hands where they're locked around my hips and I explode, crying out twice as loud as I did when he used the vibrator on me.

The first orgasm I had with Ivan was the wildest and strongest of my life.

The second replaces it completely.

I'm starting to worry that I might not survive a third.

Even before I'm done panting and shaking, Ivan loses his last shred of patience. He climbs on top of me and thrusts that thick, gorgeous cock inside of me.

I've never felt a sensation quite like it. His cock is like steel encased in velvet. It fits inside me like it was made for me, like its only purpose is to give me pleasure in exactly the ways I want.

I think Ivan Petrov is in the wrong business.

He should make a mold of himself and sell it to women worldwide.

I've hardly amused myself with that thought before I'm flushed through with jealousy at the very idea.

I found this perfect specimen, and I want to keep him all for myself.

Ivan slings my limp legs over his shoulders. He plows into me with all his strength. His whole body flexes as he drives deep inside of me, grunting like a beast.

He kisses my mouth, my throat, my breasts. He's touching me in a dozen places at once, attacking the whole of my body with his. He's letting out every ounce of that frustration and rage that was bottled up inside of him.

I've never been overpowered like this.

I usually fight to maintain control.

But with Ivan, I don't want to fight. I don't want to struggle.

I let myself be swept away by him, consumed by him. I don't feel frightened or confined. Paradoxically, it's freeing in a way I've never experienced before. For once I don't have to plan or take action. All I have to do is go along with it, experience it.

He's the brush and I'm the paint. He's the wind and I'm the bird.

He's bringing me to climax once more. This time I don't clench or squirm or try to hold it back in any way. I just let the pleasure surge through every cell of my body.

He wraps me up in his arms. He crushes me against his body until I can't move at all. The only thing moving is his cock, sliding in and out of me, inch by inch. He squeezes me tighter and tighter as he erupts inside of me. I can't breathe from how tight he's holding me, and yet I don't want him to let go.

And he doesn't, not even after he finishes. We lay together on that shitty old mattress, with his arms enveloping me.

Only then do I remember that I'm locked in a cell with this man. That I was planning to escape.

Ivan seems to remember the same thing.

He lets go of me and says, "Do you want to come upstairs and take a shower?"

I can't help my look of surprise and suspicion.

"Come upstairs?"

"Yeah. I thought you'd want to get cleaned up."

His tone is as gruff as ever, but I see the way he's looking at me, watching my face, waiting to see if I'll accept his offer.

He's trying to be kind to me.

How odd.

"Uh, okay," I say.

I'm not going to turn down his offer. I've been washing off in the sink, but that's not the same thing as a proper shower with shampoo.

However, now that Ivan's ripped my underwear, I don't have a single stitch of clothing.

Ivan seems to realize the same thing.

"Take my shirt," he says, throwing it to me.

Interesting. He doesn't care if his men see me coming upstairs —but he doesn't want them to see me naked.

I put on his dress shirt, which smells like his warm skin and his cologne. The scent sends a little shiver down my legs. I button it up, using the few buttons that remain after I tore it off him. He's so much bigger than me that the shirt hangs down to mid-thigh, the cuffs covering my hands.

Even though we just finished fucking, Ivan stares at me in his shirt, his eyes roving down my bare legs. He likes the way I look in it.

He pulls on his trousers, then walks over to the door to open the lock with his fingerprint.

I expect him to give me a warning—tell me not to try anything stupid once we're out of the cell. But he doesn't say anything at all.

Whatever happened to him tonight, he's obviously got bigger worries than me running away.

# 12

## IVAN

I lead Sloane up to the main floor, past the dining hall where nearly all my men are drinking and talking quietly, despite the lateness of the hour. They're mourning Karol.

I should be in there with them. But when I got back from the club, I couldn't speak to anyone. I was in such a state of bottled-up fury that I had to fight or fuck or run.

I went down to the catacombs in a daze. I flung open the door and saw Sloane waiting for me.

She knew what I needed better than I did.

And she gave it to me, immediately.

She flushed out all the rage and frustration that was poisoning my mind.

Now I can think clearly at last.

The first thing I know is that I'm not going all the way down to the dungeon to see her. She's staying in my room from now on. I'll still lock her in, but I no longer believe she's going to try to murder me in my sleep. And if she does, I guess I deserve it.

It's my fault Karol is dead. I sent him to watch Remizov. He wasn't ready for a job like that. That mistake is on my head.

As I let Sloane into my suite, I can see her looking around in that curious, appraising way I'm already starting to recognize. She surveys the tobacco-colored couches, the fireplace large enough to roast an ox, the plush rugs, the black and white Robert Frank prints on the wall.

"Does this meet with your approval?" I ask her. "Will it bump up my Airbnb rating just a little?"

She laughs softly. It's the first time I've heard her laugh. I don't want to admit what an effect it has on me—lifting my spirits that were sunk so low that they were almost subterranean.

"Yes," she says. "You're well on your way to four stars."

"Four," I snort. "Try the shower before you say that."

I lead her into the bathroom. It's the most modern part of the whole compound—all spotless white marble and gleaming steel, with heated towel racks, a full-body dryer, and a shower that could comfortably fit four people. There are six separate faucets, including one that pours ready-mixed soap suds.

I turn them all on for her, just a shade hotter than comfortable.

The bathroom fills with steam.

Without a trace of shyness, Sloane strips off my shirt and stands naked before me once more. I've never been one to chase after the modest girls. But this woman has confidence on a level I've never seen. She's intelligent. Capable. Ruthless.

She's just like me.

Is it narcissistic to say that I love that about her?

I've never considered tying myself to any woman, not permanently. But if I did, it would have to be a woman like this. A true equal.

Of course, that's all theoretical.

I don't have time for romance, especially not now.

Still, I can't help staring at Sloane as she steps into the shower and starts languorously soaping her body. She runs her hands over her wet, slippery breasts, down the flat plane of her stomach.

She tilts her head back to work a handful of shampoo into her hair, her lifted chin revealing the long curve of her throat. Her arched back makes her figure look all the more alluring.

I hadn't planned to join her, but it's more than I can resist.

I drop my trousers once more and join her.

"You missed a spot," I say, sliding my palms over the curves of her ass.

"You're right," she purrs. "I'm completely filthy."

Before I know what I'm doing, I'm kissing her again. My cock is rising to attention, my balls tingling as if they haven't had release in weeks, instead of less than twenty minutes ago.

I notice that when Sloane stands on tiptoe and puts her arms around my neck, she's the perfect height to reach up and kiss me. And when I clasp my hands under her ass, it's the easiest thing in the world to lift her up, with her legs wrapped around my waist.

I lower her down onto my cock, fucking her under the steaming hot shower spray. We're still kissing, our mouths locked together and our tongues moving in rhythm.

It's so easy to hold her up. She's strong, and she's using her legs and arms to ride me at the same time that I'm thrusting upward into her.

I find myself looking into her eyes, which are dark in color but bright in expression. She really does remind me of a little fox: quick and wild and clever.

We have dark-colored foxes in Russia—their coats are black in the summer, silver in the winter. They're rare and valuable, just like Sloane.

I carry her out of the shower, over to the bed. I pull her onto my lap, so I can watch those beautiful, natural tits bouncing on top of me. I lay back against the pillows.

She rolls her hips in a slow, steady rhythm, like she's riding a horse. Her eyes are closed and her lips are parted. She raises her arms to push back her dark curls, the droplets of water from her wet hair pattering down onto the bed.

She's squeezing my cock with each roll of her hips. Her skin is flushed from the hot water, and from the pleasure of this position. I can see the little nub of her clit grinding against my lower abdomen.

She leans forward and lays her palms flat on my chest, to increase the friction against her clit. Now she's grinding harder and harder, like a mortar and pestle.

I'm determined to let her cum first, but it's impossible to hold back. She's squeezing me so forcefully. If I look at her, the sight of those gorgeous breasts swaying above my face will put me over the edge. But if I close my eyes, the sensation of her riding my cock is all the more intense.

Jesus, I can't win. I can feel my balls contracting, my cock pulsing.

Luckily, Sloane is right on the edge too. It seems like she was waiting for me. As soon as I start to cum, I can feel her shaking on top of me. Her pussy clenches around my cock in one long squeeze, and it makes me go off like a cannon, an orgasm that barrels out of me, that sends sparks flashing across my closed eyelids.

This girl is going to give me a stroke.

I can't think, speak, hear, or feel anything but that pure ecstatic surge.

And then I'm back inside my body again, with Sloane lying beside me, her head on my chest.

It's a position that makes a man want to tell a woman his deepest, darkest secrets.

And Sloane wants to hear them.

Because she's asking, "What happened today?"

Before I can consider what a terrible idea it is to tell her anything, I'm opening my mouth and spilling it all out.

I tell Sloane about Remizov, about how he's been expanding his empire in St. Petersburg, and how he seems to have the police and the politicians in his pocket. And then, though I can't believe I'm admitting it, I tell her what happened to Karol, and that it's my fault. I tell her I've been outmaneuvered and outsmarted.

It's insane for me to admit any of this. Forget about safety or prudence—I want to impress Sloane. I don't want to show her my weakness and failure.

But I tell her everything.

Because she's a professional.

She knows that in our world, things go wrong.

She knows better than anyone that it's kill or be killed, every day.

And that's why I want her advice.

When I finish speaking, she lays there quietly for a minute, pondering over everything I've said.

If she were a normal person, she'd probably try to say something comforting, like it wasn't my fault that Karol got caught, even though we'd both know that was bullshit.

But Sloane is not a normal person.

She says, "The box at the gate was bait. The guns in the warehouse are bait as well."

"I know that," I say.

"But you still want them back."

"Sure. If I can get them."

"Well, take a page out of Remizov's book. Capture a couple of his men. Make them get the guns for you."

I consider this. It's not a terrible idea. If Remizov has some trap in place—like some of Utkin's officers waiting to arrest me—then it's his goons that will get pinched, not mine.

"Not a bad idea," I say. "What about Remizov himself?"

"That's a trickier problem. You don't know where he lives? He doesn't have a monastery of his own?" she asks with a teasing edge to her tone.

"Not that I've found."

"Does he have a mother or brother he loves?"

"Not that I know of."

"A girlfriend?"

"If he has a girlfriend, I doubt he gives a fuck about her. He strikes me as a bit of a sociopath."

"Hmm. Retaliation is going to be tricky then. It's easiest to get people at home."

"That's true," I say to Sloane. "As long as you don't come clomping into their room so loud that you wake them up."

"Oh, shut up!" she says. "You're the first person that ever woke up. You've got a guilty conscience—or the ears of a bat. Now do you want my help or not?"

"I do," I tell her, with a pretend expression of contrition.

I can't help teasing her, but I'm being sincere. I want to hear what she thinks.

"You're used to being the strongest person in a fight," she tells me. "That's why you want to attack him head-on."

"He's not stronger than me," I protest. "He may have made some alliances, but—"

She cuts me off.

"It doesn't matter if you could take him in a fair fight," she says. "He's not going to play fair. And even if he did, and even if you won, you're going to lose a lot of men."

That's true. I have a vision of two armies facing each other, taking turns firing at each other with their muskets. It's a stupid way to fight.

Sloane taps the nail of her index finger against her bottom teeth.

"Let's put aside the idea of revenge, just for the moment," she says. "Instead of trying to kill Remizov outright, how can you weaken him? You want to cut him a hundred times with a poisoned blade, before you strike the fatal blow."

"I can't just attack his businesses and supply lines outright. He's got the commissioner and the governor on his side."

"No," Sloane agrees. "You'll have to get creative. But that will be better anyway, psychologically speaking. If you can destroy his assets one by one, without him even being sure who's done it or how, that's going to put him in a worse state anyway."

I think of my men downstairs. My brother, cousins, friends since childhood.

"He doesn't have a family," I say, thinking out loud. "His men are all hired."

"That's right," Sloane says. "They're not actually loyal to him. He pays them. And they might be afraid of him. But the bond isn't as strong."

I think of his actions so far. One of his first moves was the raid on the diamond district. He needed money.

"Find his cash and you can bleed him out," Sloane says. "Without money, he'll lose his men."

"You are a clever little fox," I growl in her ear, pulling her even closer against me. "You should give up your job as the grim reaper and come work for me."

I feel her stiffen.

"I don't work for anyone," she says. Her voice is cold. I've offended her.

"I know," I say quickly. "Of course you don't. I wouldn't want to, either."

She relaxes, ever so slightly.

But she's still on her guard.

I stroke her hair, which is still damp and smells nicely of my shampoo. I use long, slow, heavy strokes with my fingers. I'm deliberately soothing and quieting her. I want her to sleep next to me tonight.

I can feel her body growing warmer and heavier. Her breathing slowing.

"You want to stay here with me?" I ask her, my voice barely more than a whisper.

"Mm hmm," she says, nuzzling all the closer against me.

I probably should, at the very least, remove all the guns from the room.

But I'm just as drained and relaxed as Sloane.

In this moment, there's almost nothing that could pull me away from this bed, and the woman lying in my arms.

## 13

SLOANE

*Foxes are hunters, but they don't rely on brute strength. They're subtle and clever. Fond of outwitting others.*

— LISA KLEYPAS

I wake to the sound of ice cubes shifting inside a glass, silverware clinking against a plate. I sit up in a bed far larger, warmer, and softer than the one I've been inhabiting lately.

The room is full of daylight. It streams in through a bank of windows on the right-hand wall—windows nearly as tall as I am, narrow and rectangular and topped with a Gothic arch.

Ivan is no longer in bed beside me. But I hear him moving around in the adjoining room. I'm already coming to know the sound of his heavy tread, his methodical movements.

I roll off the bed and grab a silk robe that hangs over the back of the nearest chair. I put it on, tying the belt at the waist.

I pad barefoot across the carpet, through the doorway to the sitting room with its hefty leather furniture and its massive fireplace.

Ivan is standing in front of that fireplace, arranging several dishes on a portable rolling table—the type they use in hotels. The table is covered in a linen tablecloth, and it's carrying an array of breakfast foods, including a large platter of fresh-baked pastries, a bowl of fruit, bacon, sausages, a carafe of orange juice, a samovar of hot coffee, and dishes and glassware for two people.

"Nice spread," I say approvingly.

"Still trying to earn that fifth star," Ivan says.

He pulls up a seat for me—one of the heavy, extraordinarily comfortable leather armchairs. I sink down into it, reaching at once for the coffee.

The smell of the food is almost making me drool. I've barely eaten in the last thirty-six hours. Ivan probably would have brought me something sooner if I'd asked, but we were a little . . . distracted.

Well . . . he did bring me some oatmeal. A flush rises in my cheeks, remembering that particular meal.

Ivan is thinking the same thing. He gives me a wicked smile and says, "Don't worry. This time I brought you a fork."

I look him in the eye and grin.

"I don't know if that's an improvement," I tell him. "I rather liked the service at my last meal."

Our eyes are locked across the table, the food forgotten yet again. I know he wants to tumble back into the bed as badly as I do.

But he's already dressed in a charcoal-gray suit. He's got work to do today.

Ivan sees me glance down at his jacket and trousers.

"I've got to go out," he says, confirming my thoughts. "I took your ideas from last night. Added a few of my own."

I nod my head slowly. For some reason, the thought of Ivan leaving the compound on his mission of revenge against Remizov is frightening to me. Why should I care about some Bratva battle for territory in St. Petersburg? Why should I care if Ivan gets himself killed? I was about to do it myself, two days ago.

Yet I do care.

God, I'm so annoyed with myself.

My father was my only family and my only friend for almost the whole of my childhood. He was everything to me.

Then I realized he was out of his mind. His mission was madness. And my world came crashing down.

I swore to myself that I wasn't going to put myself in that position again. I wasn't going to tie my emotions to someone guaranteed to smash them into pieces. Really, I didn't plan to get attached to anyone at all.

But, despite my intentions, I like Ivan. I respect him. And I'm attracted to him on a level I never thought possible.

Still, I don't want to get drawn into his vendetta against Remizov.

My job is dangerous, but it's impersonal.

Ivan's hatred for Remizov is extremely personal.

So are my feelings for Ivan.

None of these things should mix.

Ivan is watching my face, trying to guess the thoughts that are spinning around and around in my head.

He has a hesitant, almost hopeful expression.

Does he want to ask me to come with him today?

Does he think because we were strategizing last night, that means I'm on his team now?

No. That's not happening. I'm not on any team.

I sit back in my chair, putting a little more space between Ivan and me. I add a splash of cream to my coffee and stir it, keeping my eyes on the mug so I don't have to look at the gorgeous man sitting across from me.

"Well, good luck today," I tell him, trying to keep my voice casual. "Don't get yourself killed. But if you do, maybe make it look like I did it. I could still get my bonus."

"I'll do my best," Ivan says.

His tone is light. Still, I hear the edge of disappointment. He's not asking for my help because he already knows I'll say no.

He finishes the glass of water in front of his plate. He's eaten a little bacon, but not much else. He's keyed up. Anxious about the day ahead of him.

"I'll see you later, then," he says.

"Right."

I glance around the sitting room, which is stuffed with bookshelves. So many that I would think this was the library, if I hadn't already seen the one out in the hall.

"You have any books in English?" I ask him. "I don't read Cyrillic very well."

I can read it, but it's not as relaxing for me.

"Yes," Ivan says. "Over on that shelf."

He points to the bookcase on the left-hand side of the fireplace, stuffed with a mixture of paperbacks and hardcovers.

"Read anything you like," Ivan says.

"Thanks," I say. "Well. See you."

Ivan nods. He seems like he wants to say something else to me, but he doesn't actually open his mouth. He just stands there looking me over from the crown of my head to the tip of my toes. His eyes are so dark and stern that his look has the same effect on me as if he were running his rough, strong hands over every inch of me.

I want to say something else to him myself. What, precisely, I have no idea.

Maybe, *I've never met anyone quite like you.*

Maybe, *Can you please explain this insane effect you're having on me?*

Maybe, *Don't go. Stay here with me.*

Instead, I just say, "Ivan. Seriously—be careful."

He nods, his broad jaw firmly set.

"I will," he says.

And then he's gone.

I watch out the window. I see his men gathering in the yard, and then, a short time later, Ivan joining them. They get into three separate unmarked SUVs and drive through the tall stone pillars, away from the compound. The iron gates close behind them.

Ivan left with nine men, including his brother Dominik.

From what I've observed in my short stint prowling around the monastery, and passing the dining hall on two separate occasions, Ivan has eleven soldiers living here, besides himself. He used to have twelve, but then Remizov killed Karol—the boy I saw sleeping on the couch. The one wearing the orange running shoes.

That means that Ivan only left two guards behind today.

Which means I have an excellent opportunity to make my escape.

The funny thing is, I'm not particularly inclined to leave. I no longer think Ivan is going to kill me. And despite my teasing him, his hosting skills really are improving by the day.

Would it be so bad to lounge around his suite, reading his books, snooping through his stuff, eating more of the ridiculous amount of food he brought up for our breakfast?

When he comes back—*if he comes back* . . . WHEN he comes back, he can tell me how things went with Remizov. What he's planning to do next.

And he can throw me down on his bed once more and ravage my body in that aggressive, voracious way that no man before him has managed to match.

That sounds nice, doesn't it?

Unfortunately, I've never been very good at accepting what would be nicest and most comfortable for myself.

I always seem to do things the hard way.

I like Ivan. But I'm not ready to be his little pet.

So I start circling the master suite, searching for my way out.

I try the door first, of course.

It's locked—not a particularly secure lock, but one that is alarmed and will surely send an alert to Ivan's phone if I open it.

Now that I'm in a fully-stocked room instead of a cell, I have a lot more tools at my disposal—for instance, I'm sure Ivan's got plenty of weapons squirreled away in here. But if I were to shoot the lock off the door, that would make a lot of noise. Enough to bring one or both of those remaining guards running.

And whatever I do, I don't want to hurt any of Ivan's men. Two days ago, I wouldn't have cared. But now I know this is a family. I'm not interested in making an enemy out of any of them.

Ivan's suite has windows on two sides. I can see the whole north and west sides of the compound from here. Specifically, I can see the roofs and stone walls. Ivan's suite is almost the highest point of the monastery, other than two towers on the opposite side.

However, these windows aren't a good point of egress. The original glass has been removed. The new glass includes tamper sensors and steel-wire reinforcement. They don't open —I'd have to smash the glass and cut the wire. Again, tripping alarms.

But . . . there's another way.

That massive fireplace.

Original to the monastery. Big enough to fit several of me inside its flue.

That's my way out of here.

But first, clothes.

I raid Ivan's closet, looking for the smallest clothing I can find. The vast majority of what he owns is suits, and even his casual clothes are miles too big for me. But beggars can't be choosers. The same for thieves.

I take a dark gray hoodie, and a pair of black joggers. I roll up the pantlegs and the sleeves and cinch the drawstring of the pants as tight as I can. I take socks too. I plan to use several pairs, because there's no way I'm going to be able to keep my feet inside any of Ivan's shoes, but then I see my own soft leather climbing shoes lined up neatly next to Ivan's Oxfords.

Lady Luck is with me. Maybe Ivan planned to give them back to me. Not that I'm holding my breath on him being motivated to give me any kind of clothes—he was enjoying the alternative too much.

Smiling to myself, I slip on my familiar shoes once more.

Now, I have a slight dilemma—though I saw from the yard that it was no longer snowing, it's still going to be frigidly cold. However, if I put on too much bulk, I won't be as maneuverable.

After some debate, I decide to wear only the hoodie and keep myself warm by running.

Which means I'm ready to go.

I pull aside the grate. Then I step inside Ivan's massive fireplace.

Fortunately, he didn't light it this morning. If he had, I would have had to wait for the stone to cool, which might have taken all day.

I brace my feet against one side of the flue, my palms against the other. I begin to shimmy upward in the plank position.

It's not too bad at first. The large, rough stones provide plenty of purchase. And it's airy enough that I'm not choking on soot.

However, the very spaciousness of its dimensions soon begins to cause problems for me. If the chimney were smaller, I could brace my back against the wall and climb with my legs alone. But I'm stretched out to my fullest length, in a position that's difficult to hold, let alone to climb upward.

Besides that, the bizarre exertions of the last few days have exhausted me. I feel like I've been a captive for weeks instead of barely two days. I feel winded and shaky before I've barely started.

Also, I wish I weren't looking down. The farther I climb, the longer the drop below me becomes. If my hands slip, if I lose my strength, I'm going to crash down onto a pile of logs that is anything but forgiving. I should have dragged some bedding or a pile of towels into the bottom of the chimney to break my fall.

But that would be planning for failure. I'm counting on success.

I'm not going to give up. Inch by inch I'm going to work my way up, like a reverse Santa Clause.

Thankfully, the chimney is becoming slightly narrower the higher up I climb. I'm also starting to pass the tangled mats of abandoned birds' nests, and I see more and more daylight shining on my pale, filthy arms.

Finally, I reach the top. By now the flue is narrow enough that I can brace myself, which is lucky because I need all my strength to wrench off the grate over the chimney top.

And then I've done it. I'm pulling myself up onto the roof of the monastery.

The roof is steeply pitched, slippery with snow and ice. It's a long way down to the frozen dirt of the yard.

It's a bit of an "out of the frying pan, into the fire" situation—if the fire was freezing cold and windy. Inside the chimney I was protected from the wind. Now I feel like it's trying to push me off the roof.

Well, the longer I stand here, the colder I'm going to get. I start making my way toward the northwest corner of the roof—it's the point I spotted from the window, where the corner of the roof is closest to the walls encircling the monastery.

I'm hoping to jump from the roof to the wall. It's a jump I couldn't have made in the opposite direction. But since the roof is higher than the wall, gravity will be my friend.

I'm so focused on my destination that I don't even notice when my feet slip out from under me. All I know is that I'm suddenly down on my ass, sliding toward the edge of the roof, gaining speed by the moment. I'm hurtling down like a toboggan, my fingers scrabbling uselessly against the slick metal. I can't slow down at all, can't catch hold of anything.

I feel the sickening sense of weightlessness as my body goes hurtling off the edge of the roof. With one last desperate clutch, I manage to grab the very edge of the roof and hang on with my fingertips, my legs dangling down.

Fuck, that was close.

I have now become one of those posters with the kitten dangling from the wire.

*Just Hang in There, Baby.*

I try to pull myself up again, but I'm so goddamned tired from the climb up the chimney.

My father used to make me do dozens of push-ups and pull-ups. Once I could do ten strict pull-ups in a row, he added a weighted belt around my waist. That's what it feels like now—like I have a massive weight pulling me down. But it's just my own exhausted flesh.

My arms are shaking, my fingertips cramping. Slowly I pull myself up so I'm standing on the edge of the roof once more.

And now I'm looking across an eight-foot gap to the top of the old stone wall. The gap looks a lot wider from this perspective, and the wall a lot narrower.

Staring between the two is not boosting my morale.

"You're committed now, you idiot," I mutter to myself.

I scrabble back up the roof a little way to give myself a running start. Then I sprint down the slope as fast as I can and launch myself into the air.

# 14

## IVAN

Andrei calls my phone just as I'm parking my Hummer in an alleyway behind the Deutsche Bank.

I already have a good idea what he's calling about, but I pick up the phone anyway.

"What is it?" I say, brusquely.

"It's the girl," he says. "She's escaping over the back wall. What do you want me to do?"

Andrei means, should he shoot her, or just capture her and bring her back.

I knew this was the likely outcome of leaving Sloane alone in my room, which is not nearly as secure as the basement cells.

But still, I feel an unreasonable stab of disappointment. I had hoped she wouldn't want to run away. Or at least, not so soon.

I should have known better.

"Just let her go," I say to Andrei.

There's a pause. Then he says, confused, "Let her go?"

"You heard me!" I bark at him.

"Right, of course," he says. "You got it, boss."

I hang up the phone, my face hot.

Sloane was a prisoner. Of course she was going to run the minute she got the chance.

Still, I can't help feeling like she abandoned me.

What else did I expect?

Nothing. I didn't expect anything from her.

But stupidly, I hoped.

There's no time to worry about it now. We're on Volynskiy Pereulok, close to the Church of the Savior on the Spilled Blood. Dom says that Remizov has a safe deposit box at this bank.

We haven't figured out exactly which box is his. So, we're going to rob them all.

As I suspected, when we spied on Remizov's operations at the diamond district, we saw that he now has several uniformed cops standing guard. They're not involved in the sale of the gemstones, but it's clear that Remizov is operating with their tacit approval, under their protection.

I'm amazed at the blatant control he's securing over the St. Petersburg police. It's not as if the cops haven't taken bribes to turn a blind eye before, but this is police collaboration on a whole new level.

I've met with the heads of the St. Petersburg branches of the Sidarov, Nikitin, and Markov families. Only the Markovs were willing to join my men today. Olaf Sidarov openly admitted that he's already allied himself with Remizov, and Eli Nikitin said he wanted to remain neutral for the time being—which means he wants to see which way the wind is blowing so he can attach himself to the apparent winner.

If that winner is me, Nikitin is very wrong to think I'm going to forget his cowardice and disloyalty.

Hedeon Markov, by contrast, is an old gangster who's never kissed the ring of anyone in this city. He's as stubborn as a mule. Today I love him for that.

He's sent me four men to add to my nine, including his son Kristoff. Kristoff is as fat and grumpy as his father, but I've heard that he once took down four men in a bar fight, and half the walls in the bar as well. So I'm glad to have his scowling bulk next to me.

I've also got Alter Farkas, whose wife and daughters were killed by Remizov's men in the raid on the diamond district. He's even older than Hedeon Markov, and no fighter, but he has information that will be useful to me today.

I divide my men into three groups, with Markov and Farkas's men parceled out amongst them. I'm not taking any chances on double-crossing. I've instructed Dom and the others that no one texts or calls anybody until after our work is done.

We split up to hit three places at once—the bank, the diamond district, and the customs office where Remizov has been usurping the Stepanov's drug smuggling operation.

I'm handling the bank job, because it will be the most difficult.

I've got Maks with me, and Markov's son Kristoff.

We check over our weapons, then don our gloves and ski masks.

"No names," I warn the men, "and don't let anybody see your face."

Deutsche Bank has deep ties to the Russian elite. Generally speaking, it's not a place you're supposed to rob.

I have no intention of taking money from the tills or the vault —I only want the safe deposit boxes. It should be a small enough score to avoid drawing the ire of the real power players, while still cutting Remizov plenty deep.

We go over the plan several times before leaving the car.

Speed is key in any robbery. We want to be in and out in less than ten minutes, since the police will probably show up in twelve.

This branch of the Deutsche Bank is relatively small, but opulent on the exterior and interior. I can only imagine the sums of money that have passed through its vault—not to mention its computer systems. Money tracked and untracked, earned and unearned, from every country of the world.

As soon as we're through the front doors, we split up to neutralize the employees. We want to prevent them hitting any silent alarms. Maks covers the tellers, while Kristoff and I gather up the managers and staff.

There are only a few customers inside, including an old man with his grandson, and two women making deposits. Maks tells them all to sit down quietly in the corner of the room.

I'm impressed with his politeness. It's smart—calm people are easier to control. The old man seems mildly annoyed, and the two women look almost excited. They're wearing aprons over their clothes, probably having come from work at a shop or cafe. They seem pleased at the opportunity to delay their return.

The bank employees are, of course, less happy about the situation. Particularly the branch manager, who blusters and shouts.

"This is outrageous! Who do you think you are?"

"Just give us the keys to the safe deposit boxes, and we'll be on our way," I say.

"I'm not giving you any keys," the bank manager retorts stubbornly. His black hair is combed flat against his head, shiny with gel. He's wearing a blue suit, as well as rings on several fingers.

Kristoff seizes him by the lapels, lifts him in the air, and throws him across the room. The manager skids across the floor, coming to rest in front of the reception desk.

"Anybody else got keys?" Kristoff grunts.

A redheaded account manager fumbles a clutch of keys off her belt.

"H-here," she stammers, holding them out to Kristoff. "Use mine."

I take the keys and head down to the safe deposit boxes.

I start opening the lock boxes, scanning their contents. I ignore the ones that hold papers, documents, photographs, and family jewelry, I'm looking only for those that contain serious cash.

Before I've gone through more than five or six, Maks comes hurrying down the stairs.

"Remizov's are twelve and thirteen," he says.

"How do you know that?"

"The little blonde teller told me," he says. I see the white flash of his teeth as he grins through the slit in his ski mask.

Even with his face covered, Maks is popular with the girls.

I unlock box twelve and thirteen.

Here's what I've been looking for—stacks of cash, piled six inches deep. I take it all, clearing the boxes bare.

I check my watch. Eight minutes gone. We're ahead of schedule.

I jog up the stairs again, my sack of cash slung over my shoulder.

"Got it," I say to Kristoff and Max.

Max tips a wink at the blonde teller. She tries to hide her smile behind her hand.

Kristoff steps over the bank manager, who's still laying in front of the desk, though I don't think he's actually hurt. He looks more like he's sulking.

We leave the bank in only eight minutes, fifty-one seconds.

We get back in the Hummer, and I drive to the rendezvous point to meet up with the other groups.

Dom returns first, with Jasha and Alter Farkas.

Despite all the police prowling the diamond district, they managed to sneak in the back of Farkas's old shop. The locks on the doors had been changed, but the safe code had not. They made off with a bag of loose stones and another hefty stack of banded hundred-dollar bills.

Farkas doesn't look pleased about the score.

"The place is going to shit already," he complains. "They haven't washed the windows once."

I give him the stones and the cash, though I know it's poor recompense for what he's lost.

"I hope to get your shop back too, before long," I tell him.

The money from the security boxes I split with the Markovs.

Kristoff hands it over to his father at once.

Hedeon tucks it in his jacket without counting it.

"That's how the Bratva do business," he says to me, with a slow nod. "As equals. With honor."

Efrem comes back with a different sort of plunder entirely—two of Remizov's men. He's got them bound and gagged in the back of his GLK.

Dom and I climb in Efrem's car for the second part of our little adventure.

We drive out to the warehouse where Remizov has been storing my guns.

Like Efrem said, there's still only two men guarding the guns, and not very well. One of them is texting on his phone when Efrem hits him from behind. The other goes down after only a cursory fight.

Dom and Efrem were right. This is much too easy.

Through the dusty windows, I can see the crates of Kalashnikovs stacked inside the warehouse. I nod for Dom to untie Remizov's kidnapped men.

Dom hauls them out of the back of the GLK, cutting his ropes.

Efrem trains his rifle on the two goons.

"Get in there and bring out our guns," he says. "And make it fast. Don't make me come in there after you."

The two guards from the warehouse are sitting next to each other on the cement, leaned up against the tires of the GLK. They glance at each other nervously as their colleagues head inside.

I hear the sound of a crate shifting, dragging.

Then an explosion rips through the warehouse.

Dom, Efrem, and I are standing back a good hundred feet, and we're still blown backward onto the cement. I tear a hole in my suit pants and scrape the shit out of my hands.

Dom stands up slowly, wiping away a streak of blood from under his nose. Efrem stares at the blast, his face glowing orange in the reflected light.

The warehouse is a fireball, which turns into a column of billowing black smoke. The guns are surely destroyed, and Remizov's men too.

Efrem looks at the two guards, tied up against the wheels of Dom's car.

"Didn't care to warn your buddies?" he says in disgust.

"I didn't know that was going to happen!" one of the men cries, staring at the flaming warehouse in shock. "Remizov just told us to stay outside."

I can see that he's thinking we might just as easily have sent him in to retrieve the guns instead.

"We'd better go," Dom says to me.

A blaze like that will draw the police and fire trucks.

"What about them?" Efrem says, nodding to the guards.

"Leave them for the cops," I say.

I can see that Efrem thinks they deserve worse than that.

But we've made it through the day without killing anyone so far. I'd like to keep it that way. I'm afraid there will be more than enough bloodshed to go around before this thing with Remizov is done.

## 15

### SLOANE

My car is still parked where I left it, the key tucked up under the wheel well. It manages to start, despite the fact that it's an old beater that's been sitting out in the snow for several days.

I always drive shitty old cars because they don't attract attention, and nobody bothers to steal them. But you do sacrifice some reliability.

The rusty Vesta coughs and sputters in a disgruntled way before it starts up. The vents spit air into my face that somehow seems even colder than the air outside, tinged with the unpleasant tang of diesel fumes.

Soon enough I'm back on the road, heading home to my safe house.

I ought to stay in a hotel for a few nights as I usually do between jobs, but I'm so extraordinarily filthy from the chimney that I'm not sure anyone would rent me a room. Besides, I'm just so, so tired. I want to be home again.

And yet, when I've stowed my car in the underground garage, and walked the four flights of stairs up to my flat, I push open the door and feel . . . underwhelmed.

My apartment seems dingy and dull after the beauty and history of Ivan's monastery. It's sterile. And quiet. And just . . . empty. There's no one here but me. No one is going to be walking through the door, crossing his arms over his broad chest and watching me with his dark eyes . . . No one's going to be joining me in my bed.

Which is fine. This is what I'm used to. This is what I've always preferred.

It never felt lonely before.

I strip off Ivan's clothes, which are not in any state to be returned to him, having gotten sooty from the chimney, torn and slushy from my slide down the roof, and then speckled with twigs and leaves from my tramp through the woods back to my car.

I'm planning to have a very long shower. But when I try to turn on the water, the shower head sputters and groans, spitting orange-tinged water, and then an irregular spray of glacial coldness.

Goddamn it. I could be standing in Ivan's steam shower right now, sudsing myself with his fancy shampoo.

I try the bathtub instead. It's an old claw-foot tub, separate from the shower. So heavy that it's cracked the tiles underneath its feet. I'd prefer a shower over a bath when I'm this dirty, but at least the tub is receiving warm water.

I stuff the plug in the drain and let the tub slowly fill. In the meantime, I pad out to the kitchen and put a kettle on to boil. I want tea, toast, and whatever else I've got in the kitchen to eat.

Ravenous, I wolf down two slices of bread while I'm waiting for another two to toast. The kettle is taking forever to boil. Impatiently, I put a teabag in my mug and check if I have any milk in the fridge.

No. No milk, and no butter for my toast.

No pretty view out my window, either. I'm on the top floor, but the only thing I can see is the iron fire escapes on either side of my flat, and the dull, flat facades of other buildings close by. Unlike Ivan's monastery, my apartment is in the heart of the city, with no lovely old trees around.

I really should move. St. Petersburg is one of the most beautiful cities in Russia—certainly the most European in style. I could have chosen a nicer neighborhood, a prettier flat. Why am I always punishing myself?

Part of it was that I never expected to stay here so long. I rented a place quickly when I was looking for my father.

The other part of it is the utilitarian way I was raised. My father taught me how to survive, not how to thrive. Not how to actually enjoy things.

But he's gone now. I'm an adult. It's up to me how I want to live, what I want to do.

For a while my goal was money. What good is money, though, when I never spend it on anything?

I don't know what I want now. Staying at Ivan's place has made me dissatisfied in more ways than one. I envy the bond he has with his men. And I'm already missing certain things about Ivan himself. Not just the sex, though god knows it's the best I've had. No, it's our other interactions I miss even more.

The way that I watch him, and he watches me every time that we speak, each of us having finally met a worthy opponent, someone worth watching, worth studying, worth trying to understand.

And the way he does understand me. When we were lying in bed together discussing Remizov, he valued my opinion.

I respect Ivan. He values intelligence, loyalty, humor.

I think at my core, I value the same things.

Which is why I regret leaving his monastery. I regret not going with him today.

I didn't have to work *for* him. But I could have worked *with* him. I could have been his friend. His partner.

The kettle begins to whistle, startling me out of my thoughts.

I pour hot water into my mug, then pick up the steeping tea, trying to use the mug to warm my hands. I'm shivering a little, naked in the chilly kitchen. I didn't want to put on my robe until I'd washed all the soot off myself.

Maybe I'll just drink the tea in the tub, so I can get in the warm water.

I take three steps in the direction of the bathroom. As I do so, I hear a sharp crash over my right shoulder. Glass shattering, as someone punches a hole in the kitchen window.

Then a heavy clunk, followed by three thuds and a roll as something is thrown in my window, skittering across the floor.

I see the battered red canister, the pin already pulled.

*Incendiary grenade.*

I drop the tea. Before the mug has even hit the floor, I'm sprinting out of the kitchen, into the bathroom. No time to try to force up the shutter of the rickety old window—I take a deep breath and make a running leap into the bathtub, which is nearly full.

The explosion rips through my apartment. I see the bright bloom of fire as all available air over my head superheats and combusts into liquid flame.

I'm lying in the bottom of the bathtub, with three feet of water over me—my only shield from the explosion. That, and the thick porcelain sides of the tub. I'm waiting for the tub to crack, the water to boil me alive.

Instead, it's the ancient wood beneath the tub that gives way.

The floorboards split, and the bathtub plummets through the ceiling of the apartment below.

I fall down into my neighbor's living room, tub and all.

Flaming plaster, wood, and tile rain down on me.

I jump out of the bathtub, bruised but not dead yet.

Now I'm standing naked in the middle of the destruction.

There's a fire raging overhead. Everything in my apartment is burning to dust.

I don't expect the rest of the floor to hold out much longer.

I look wildly around and see my neighbor, Mrs. Chugunkin, staring at me from the doorway. She's wearing her usual over-sized cardigan and carpet slippers, and she too is holding a mug of tea. She's lucky she was drinking it in the kitchen, and not on her green chintz sofa, which has been completely flattened by my bathtub.

"*Ubiraysya otsyuda!*" I shout at her. *Get out of here!*

We race for her front door, Mrs. Chugunkin getting there first, because I stop to snatch another wooly cardigan off the coatrack in her hallway. I shove my feet into a pair of her rain boots, and then we run out the door, down the hallway, and all the way down the four flights of stairs to the ground floor.

By this time, we're in a crowd of apartment dwellers who have heard the explosion and are trying to flee the building. I see the superintendent, Mr. Bobrov, trying to direct people but almost getting trampled by the plumber who lives on the second floor.

"What was it?" Mrs. Chugunkin says to me in confusion. "Was it a gas leak?"

I ignore her, pushing past her to the doorway down to the parking garage.

I avoid my own ancient Vesta and hot-wire the plumber's work van instead. Whoever tossed a grenade through my window is probably well aware what kind of car I drive. They probably saw me pull in. They must have been close by, watching and waiting for me to arrive back home.

What I don't know is who's trying to kill me.

Is it Remizov, in retaliation for failing to complete the hit on Ivan?

He's not supposed to know who he hired to do the job, any more than I'm supposed to know who hired me.

But that doesn't mean he didn't figure it out.

If I tracked Zima's IP address, that means other people can do it, too.

I start the engine of the van and pull out of the underground lot.

My first impulse is to get out of the city, head to my other safe house in Moscow. It's a shack, even shittier than this place. But I have clothes and cash stashed there, and another laptop.

That's what pisses me off the most about my apartment getting torched—it took me a long time to build my computer rig. It had all my records on it. I need it for work.

Of course, I have backups of my files in several places, plus more supplies, but all my favorite stuff was in that flat.

However, before I've driven very far out of St. Petersburg, I start thinking that switching to my other safe house isn't the best idea. After all, if somebody knew about my apartment here, they could very well know about the one in Moscow. I doubt I'll get lucky a second time if they decide to launch another grenade through my window.

I do need money, ID, and better clothes. I'm currently wearing a moth-eaten cardigan and a pair of Wellingtons.

I have emergency caches stashed in a few places around the city.

That's where I'll go first.

I'll get some money.

I'll buy some pants.

Then I'll figure out who's trying to kill me.

# 16

## IVAN

*Mist to mist, drops to drops. For water thou art, and unto water shalt thou return.*

— KAMAND KOJOURI

I've only been back at the compound an hour when Andrei calls me to tell me that a battered white van has pulled up to the gate.

When I get down there, Andrei and Vadim are flanking the van, pointing their ARs at the driver's side. I tell them to hold back, thinking that it might be rigged with explosives as well. But I can see someone sitting in the driver's seat, their hands raised.

As I walk through the gates, that person motions that they want to open the door.

I nod my head at Andrei, to tell him not to fire.

The van door creaks open.

Sloane steps out.

Whatever kind of day I've had, hers has obviously been worse.

She looks like she's been working in a coal mine—skin streaked with soot and dirt, a burn on her right forearm, and her tangled black curls twisted up in a knot on top of her head.

She's wearing some shapeless knitted cardigan over top of a cheap sweatshirt with the Russian flag on the front—the kind of sweatshirt they sell to tourists at the market stalls around the Hermitage. And then beneath that, she appears to have on men's sweatpants and a pair of gum boots.

Yet she's grinning at me, her white teeth gleaming in contrast to her filthy skin.

"Hey!" she says. "Did you miss me?"

I try to keep my face stern, since Andrei and Vadim are standing right there.

"You went to a lot of trouble to climb up the chimney, just to come right back again," I say.

Her smile falters just a little.

"Oh, you saw that, huh?"

"Obviously. There's cameras all over this place."

I nod toward the cameras stationed on every corner of the old stone walls, two of them pointing at us right now.

"Did you see the part where I almost fell off the roof?"

"Yes."

She winces, embarrassed.

In truth, that part of the video had my heart rising in my throat, though I knew from Andrei that Sloane had made it safely over the wall.

I was furious with her, watching her escape.

She could have broken her neck, when she knew damn well I would have let her go if she just asked.

Probably.

"Why are you back?" I ask her. My frustration makes my voice even gruffer than I intend it to be.

"Well," she says, her confidence wavering, "I sort of need your help."

I let out a hoot of laughter.

"You need my help?"

The absolute brass balls on this girl.

"Yeah," she says, tilting her head to the side, and smiling sweetly at me. "But don't worry. It might be useful for you, too."

I sigh.

We both know I'm going to let her inside. Making her stand in the driveway with her hands in the air is pretty pointless.

"Come on," I say, with a jerk of my head. "Andrei can bring in your . . . plumber's van."

"Thanks," she says to Andrei. "Careful with the shift—it likes to stick in second."

Andrei looks over at me, bemused. I just roll my eyes.

I stride off toward the house, Sloane tripping after me in her too-large boots. They make a ridiculous clomping sound as they stick in the muddy yard.

"So," she says. "How did your revenge go?"

"Actually," I say, wheeling around on her, "it went perfectly."

"Good!" she says, smiling up at me.

It's so fucking infuriating.

She sneaks into my house, tries to kill me, and then right when I'm starting to like her, she runs away. Then when I've decided to let her go, she's back again.

It's like she's determined to do the opposite of what I want at all times.

Which is infuriating, enraging . . .

But I must admit, at least not boring.

The last thing in the world I expected tonight was for Sloane to roll up in a plumber's van.

And now I'm extremely curious to hear what she's been up to.

We bump into Dominik coming through the front door. He stares from Sloane back to me again. And then, annoyingly, he starts grinning too.

"Hello!" Sloane says, putting out her hand. "You're the brother, right?"

"That's right," Dom says, shaking her hand and looking over at me. "And you are . . . Ivan's girlfriend? Or escaped prisoner? I always get the two confused."

"Hmm," Sloane says, also looking at me. "Unclear."

Jesus. I'm already regretting letting her inside.

"Did you eat yet?" Dom asks her.

"I could eat more," Sloane says.

"That's always my answer, too," Dom says.

I follow them into the dining hall, where Dominik gets us three plates of stroganoff, crusty black bread, and three pints of beer.

Sloane tears into her food, not seeming to care how dirty her hands are at the moment.

Dom watches her devouring the food with an expression of delight on his face. I'm not sure what he's enjoying more: Sloane herself, or how much her presence has the potential to infuriate and embarrass me.

In between massive bites of food, Sloane is giving Dom a recap of her afternoon, and me as well. She's telling it all as if it were just an amusing adventure, but hearing that an incendiary grenade went off in her kitchen, that she would have been flash-fried if the bathtub hadn't already filled, makes me sick with rage at whoever dared throw that bomb through her window.

I know it must be Remizov, but why? Because Sloane failed to kill me? Or because he knows that she and I have developed . . . whatever it is that's happening between us.

If it's the latter, then that puts a cold spike of fear into my chest.

Because Remizov has already shown how willing he is to capture and kill someone to put the screws into me.

Dom is enthralled by Sloane's narration. He's laughing and egging her on during the part about her escape from OUR compound. I don't know if I love or hate the fact that my brother likes Sloane, too. I guess it's a good thing. He's a better judge of character than I am, generally speaking.

I have to admit, I'm glad she's back. Extremely glad. More than I want to admit to myself. I'm trying not to show it on my face, but I think I might be smiling too. Not as much as Dom, but a lot more than usual.

"So anyway," Sloane says, finishing her tale, "after I grabbed some cash and guns from a cache I had in Bronevaya, I figured I should come back here. Since we now have a mutual enemy, and I have some ideas of what to do about it."

"What makes you think we need your help?" I ask Sloane rudely. It annoys me that she might only have come back here for practical reasons.

"Well," Sloane says, not rising to the bait, "I thought we could go to my broker's house together."

That surprises me.

"What for?" I ask.

"Remizov knew where I lived," Sloane says, patiently. "I assume he got that information through Zima. Which means that Zima probably has the same information about Remizov."

Huh. Not an outrageous conclusion.

"Alright," I say. "We can do that."

"*Alright*," Sloane says, imitating me, but with a ludicrously curmudgeonly tone. "*I guess I can accompany you on your brilliant lead. If I'm not too busy being stoic.*"

Dom snorts, then stops when he sees my expression. Sloane just leans over and gives me a kiss on the cheek.

Goddamnit. She was only manageable when she thought I might murder her.

"So?" Sloane says to me.

"So what?"

"Did you get the guns back?"

Now it's my turn to tell her everything that happened this afternoon.

I start out with the basic facts, but I can't help becoming more animated in response to the expression of delight on Sloane's face. She wants every last detail.

When I finish, her face is glowing with delight. She's impressed.

"I knew the warehouse was a trap!" she says. "I hope he's so pissed about the money. We've really got this fucker on the ropes."

I like the way she says "we."

"I wouldn't say he's on the ropes just yet," I say, "but I'm sure he's plenty mad."

"Ha! Good," Sloane says, taking another bite of bread and washing it down with a gulp of beer.

"So, when do you want to go to Zima's house?" I ask her.

"Why not right now?" she says, pushing away her bowl of pasta. The food has reenergized her. You would never guess that she spent her entire day running for her life.

"Why don't you take a shower first," I tell her.

She looks down, having completely forgotten the state of herself.

"Ah, right," she says.

She stands up from the table.

I'm wondering if I should follow her or not.

Then she glances back over her shoulder at me and says, "Where was your room again?"

I take her up to my suite, my hands itching to grab hold of her with every step we take. The moment the door closes behind us, I spin her around and kiss her hard on the mouth.

She responds eagerly, jumping up into my arms and wrapping her legs around my waist. We're stumbling through the room together, bumping into the end table at the foot of the couch, knocking some books onto the floor and then almost tripping over those. But I don't care, I can't stop kissing her even for a moment.

Her mouth tastes warm and inviting. Her skin smells of smoke and the outdoors—wild scents that remind me that she is my little fox, and even though she slipped her trap, she came back to me again, of her own accord.

I'm extremely glad to have her back.

But that doesn't mean I won't punish her for her naughtiness.

I sit down on the edge of the bed and then I put her over my knee. I rip down her sweatpants. There's no underwear beneath, and I give her a sharp smack on her round little buttocks.

She wriggles and squirms, beating at my legs with her fists. But I hold her tight with my left hand. With my right, I give her four more blows on her bottom until her asscheeks are glowing red.

"That's for running away," I growl at her.

She shouts, "I'll run away any time I damn well—"

I cut her off with four more blows, sharper than the ones that came before. She can't help yelping at the last few, landing on her already tender flesh.

The harder she squirms, the harder I spank her.

She's furious at me, outraged, but I know this excites her as much as it does me. This woman is wild, dangerous when she wants to be. She's been in situations that have spiked her adrenaline like the jolt of a car battery.

She's not going to get excited about boring, vanilla sex.

She needs to feel that sense of danger and dominance. Just as Sloane is my equal in intelligence and determination, she needs a man who can match her raw sexuality. This woman could never be pleasured by an accountant. She needs a fucking gangster.

I spank her until I feel the change in her body—until she's not trembling from outrage anymore, but from arousal. Her body is tuned up like a guitar string, ready to play.

If I so much as touch her in the places she's dying to be touched, she'll explode.

But I'm not done teaching her a lesson yet.

I throw her down on the bed, on all fours. Then I stand behind her, yanking her hips backward to line her up with my body. I plunge my cock inside of her.

She's so wet from the spanking that I slide right into her, all the way to the hilt, my pelvis smacking against her bottom. I grip her hips in my hand and I thrust into her over and over, fucking her hard and rough.

Her black curls have come loose from her bun. They tumble down her back and hang around her face like curtains.

The proportions of her slim little waist and her full, heart-shaped ass are unbelievably arousing. Every time I fuck her in a new position it becomes my favorite because of how luscious her body looks from each new angle.

I drive into her again and again, feeling like a wild animal myself, like a beast driven to mate. I couldn't stop if you offered me all the money in the world. I'm out of my mind with lust for this woman.

But I want to see her face, too. I want to see those dark eyes, and the way she bites her lip and bares her teeth in the throes of pleasure.

So I flip her over once more, and I climb on top of her.

And now I'm thrusting into her slower, deeper than ever. I'm pressing our bodies tight together to give her that friction I know she needs. I'm kissing the tender side of her neck, up to her earlobe, finding her most sensitive places, finding the spots that elicit each gasp and moan.

At the moment where she tips over the edge, I look in her eyes to watch it happen. To see her expression of need to turn to a look of pure bliss, as I fulfill everything she wants and desires in one all-encompassing climax.

And that's what puts me over the edge too—not her ass or her breasts or even her taste or smell. It's Sloane herself—her face and expression and voice. The way she gives herself to me.

I want to give her everything in the world in return.

# 17

## SLOANE

When Ivan and I are finished ruining his sheets, I hop into his sinfully luxurious shower once more.

Once I'm all clean, he lends me some clothes from Maks, who's shorter and slimmer than Ivan, closer to my own build. I still have to roll up the sleeves of the pullover, but I won't be tripping over the pants at least.

Nodding toward the rumpled sheets with their streaks of soot and dirt I say, "Sorry about that."

"It's fine," Ivan says. "I'll wash them later."

"You wash your own sheets?" I ask him.

It's hard to imagine this stern-looking beast of a man sorting socks and throwing a Tide Pod into the machine.

"Of course I wash my sheets," Ivan says indignantly. "I'm not some pampered prince."

"You have a chef though," I remind him.

"That's just my cousin Ori. He's Bratva too, but he's no use for anything criminal. Too timid. So he cooks for us."

I can't help laughing at that.

"So in the Petrov family, if you want to be a doctor or an accountant, you're a total disappointment to your parents."

Ivan knows I'm teasing him, but he answers my question seriously.

"Doctor or accountant would be useful. You could sew up bullet wounds. Balance the books." He pulls a sweatshirt over his head, hiding that gorgeous body of his behind dark gray cotton. "Now, if you wanted to be an astronaut..." he gives me a small smile. "We haven't expanded quite that far."

Ivan doesn't smile much, but when he does, it has quite the effect on me.

It makes my legs go wobbly and my thoughts drift off in a dozen different directions.

I feel like I need to give myself a good slap so I can focus on the task at hand.

"I need to use your computer," I tell Ivan. "To get Zima's IP address."

"I thought you already had it?" Ivan says.

"I did," I explain patiently. "But it burned up in my apartment, along with most everything else I own. It doesn't matter though—I store copies of my files remotely. I can get the address again."

"Hmm," Ivan says.

I can tell he's mildly nervous to let me touch his computer.

And he should be. In ten minutes, I could probably find everything he has stored on there and copy it too.

But I don't want to steal from Ivan.

Except maybe a few nudes . . .

"Come on," I assure him. "You can watch me the whole time."

Ivan takes me down the hall to his office, which is directly across from the library. I remember passing it on my way to Ivan's suite, the night I snuck into the monastery.

The office is a gorgeous old room, octagonal in shape, with dark wood paneling on the walls and a ceiling painted to look like a map of the world, circa 1780 or so. Australia is still New Holland. Large swathes of Africa are blank.

I see several more walls of books—even more than in Ivan's suite. I'm beginning to think Ivan is a little more scholar, a little less brute than I imagined.

"Have you read all these?" I ask him.

"No," he says honestly. "Only half."

Half is still a shit-ton of books.

I'm supposed to be going over to the computer on his desk, but I'm distracted by all these beautiful, orderly spines, neatly arranged by topic and type.

"What are your favorites?" I ask him.

"Biographies," Ivan says promptly. "Churchill. Roosevelt. Even Steve Jobs. I like to read about extraordinary people."

"My dad liked Churchill," I tell him. "He used to say 'It's hard to fail—'"

"'But it's worse never to have tried to succeed'," Ivan finishes.

"Right," I grin at him.

"My father didn't try at much. It was my mother who had the brains and the ambition."

He's looking at me in that way he has, that makes me feel stripped down, opened up, examined to my core.

"Unequal marriages lead to unhappiness," Ivan says.

"It seems like a lot of marriages lead to unhappiness," I reply, keeping my eyes on the books on the shelf.

That was certainly true of my parents. Ivan's as well, it sounds like.

"Do you think it has to be that way?" Ivan asks.

I glance back over at him.

His arms look harder than steel, folded across his broad chest. His expression is so determined, that I can't imagine Ivan failing at anything, ever.

"No," I say at last. "I guess I'm on team 'it's better to try.'"

I want to kiss him again. That's all I want to do, whenever we're in a room alone together.

"What's it like growing up in a mafia family?" I ask him.

"Strange," Ivan says. "I went to a normal school, with the children of teachers and lawyers and bankers, and a few other Bratva. As soon as anyone hears your name, they think they already know everything about you. And in some ways, they're right. I've always fulfilled what was expected of me."

"Did you ever want to do anything else?" I say.

"Sure," Ivan nods. He lists them off on his fingers: "Rugby star. Actor. Astronaut. They were only childish fantasies, though. I was Bratva. And I never wanted anything else. Until . . . very recently."

I can feel my skin burning.

I know exactly what it feels like to think you're content, that you don't need anything. And then to realize there's something you need so badly that you can't think how you ever lived without it . . .

I'm not ready to admit to that just yet, however.

So, I sit down at Ivan's desk, sinking into his leather chair, smelling the intoxicating scent of his cologne that has permeated the material.

I open up his laptop and remote into my encrypted server, which is disguised as a website about birdwatching. I access my files and find Zima's IP address, which, after a little more digging, I connect to an actual street address in Tsentralny.

Ivan is watching my fingers fly around on the keyboard with an expression of amazement.

"Where did you learn to do all that?" he asks.

"My father kept me in the house a lot," I tell him. "He was paranoid about me going out anywhere. But there's no limit to where you can go online."

I write the address out on a scrap of paper from Ivan's desk.

"You want to take my plumber's van?" I ask him.

I'm mostly joking, but Ivan shrugs and says, "Might as well. It blends in."

I let Ivan drive so I can plug the address into the van's ancient GPS. I'm amazed how easily he handles the stubborn gear shift. When I was driving, the van jerked along like a go-cart. Ivan manages to pull smoothly through the gates, and down the long, shady drive back to the main road.

"You like living out of the city?" I ask him.

Ivan nods.

"I'd live all the way out in the country, if it wasn't bad for business."

This man is such a paradox to me. A scholar and a gangster. Retiring and ambitious.

I should have realized that from the start. What he's supposed to do and what he actually wants to do are different. Or else Ivan would have just killed me the moment we met.

Before long, we've arrived at the street where Zima supposedly lives. However, the address I've tracked down isn't a house at all—it's a restaurant. Ivan and I take a quick walk around the exterior of the building to see if there's an apartment attached, but it appears to simply be a normal cafe, closed for the night.

"You think he works out of this place?" Ivan asks, eyeing the turned-over chairs atop the tables, visible through the plate-glass windows of the cafe. "Or is the address just wrong?"

"I'm not sure . . ." I say.

I walk around the side of the building once more, and that's when I spot it—an Ethernet cable hard-wired into the box on the side of the building. It's hidden in the jumble of gas and electric meters, behind the large garbage bins overflowing with bags of trash.

The cable stretches across the alleyway, into the building next door.

"See." I point it out to Ivan. "He's tapping into their internet."

"And look at this," Ivan says. He's followed the cable to the basement apartment of the building next door. "Somebody already broke the lock."

I can see that the deadbolt has shattered through the wood. The door has been hastily repaired and a new lock added, but the damage to the doorframe remains.

"Should I knock?" I say to Ivan in a low voice.

"No, I think whoever was here before had the right idea," Ivan says.

He turns his shoulder to the door and barrels toward it like a bull. There's a sharp snap as the doorframe breaks again, and Ivan's momentum carries him inside.

I follow after him into the dank little apartment.

It's dingy and crowded, and it stinks of dirty laundry and unwashed dishes. Considering that Zima takes a fifteen percent commission for brokering hits, I'm surprised he can't afford a nicer place. Or a maid.

Half-eaten fast-food containers are scattered everywhere. I can see his computer rig in the middle of the living room—there, at least, he's spent some money. He's got half a dozen monitors and all the fanciest accessories for gaming set up around a nicely padded chair that looks like the captain's seat in a spacecraft.

But Zima himself is nowhere to be seen. I'm thinking he must have fled after Remizov's men paid him a visit. Until I hear Ivan's bemused voice saying, "Is this him?"

I follow Ivan into the bedroom. I see a towel tacked up over the window in place of curtains. A mattress on the floor, with no bed frame. And a teenage boy tangled up in a blanket.

"You've got to be shitting me," I say.

Ivan pokes the kid with the toe of his boot.

The kid startles awake, his eyes red and bleary, his hair sticking up in all directions.

"What?" he says, and then when he sees us, "Oh, shit."

"Oh, shit is right," I tell him. "Are you Zima?"

"Uh, yeah," he says, sheepishly. "I mean, it's Afanasi, actually, but Zima is like my code name."

Ivan makes a strangled noise that sounds suspiciously like a laugh.

"What in the holy fuck are you doing brokering hits?" I demand. "What are you, twelve years old?"

"I'm eighteen," Zima says, as if that's any better.

I seize him by the hair and drag him out of bed. Zima is wearing only a pair of old and sagging underpants. He yelps and slaps at my hand, but I pull him easily over to his computer station.

I throw him down in the chair.

"Did you tell Remizov where I live?" I demand.

"Well," Zima says, eyeing Ivan nervously, "yeah. Kinda. I told his goons."

I want to pop him right in the mouth for that. But I refrain. For the moment.

"That's fine," I say, through gritted teeth. "Now you can return the favor and tell me where he lives."

"Uh, I don't know if I should," Zima says.

"You definitely should," Ivan says, his voice lower and rougher than ever. "Because if you don't, I'm going to break your fingers one by one. Which will make it difficult to type."

I glance over at Ivan, mildly annoyed.

"I can threaten him myself," I say.

Ivan raises one eyebrow.

"Alright," he says. "Go ahead, then."

"Listen, you little shit," I say, grabbing Zima by the throat, "I got a grenade through my window because of you. I know if you figured out where I live, you did the same to Remizov. So spill it."

"Alright, alright!" Zima says, holding up his hands. "Here."

He picks up his phone off the desk and types something.

"There," he says. "I just texted it to you."

"You have my phone number too?" I shriek.

Zima shrugs.

"Yeah," he says.

I check my phone and confirm that Zima sent the address.

It's there alright.

But there's one thing bothering me.

I have a strong inclination to kill this kid, so he doesn't give out my information to anybody else. I'm not going to do it, but the temptation is there.

Which makes me wonder why Remizov let him live once he'd gotten my address.

"Hey," I say to Zima. "How come Remizov didn't kill you?"

"Oh," Zima says. "I mean, I totally thought he was going to. But I told him I'd get the flash drive back."

"What flash drive?"

"Well, it was bullshit. I don't actually know where it is. But you probably do?" Zima asks hopefully.

I'm staring at him in total confusion. Until I remember the flash drive I took off Yozhin at the Raketa strip club.

"Wait," I say, "are you talking about that job with Yozhin?"

"Yeah," Zima says, as if it's the most obvious thing in the world.

"How does Remizov know about the flash drive?"

"He knows about it," Zima says, slowly and distinctly like I'm a total idiot, "because it's his drive."

A whole lot of things are flipping position in my head right now.

"Pull up Remizov's file," I say to Zima.

Zima types on his computer and Remizov's file pops up, complete with a color headshot of a sickly-looking man with pale blue eyes and extraordinarily thin lips.

The man in the black suit.

The one from the club.

I'm shaking my head, agreeing with Zima that I am, indeed, an idiot. This whole time I assumed Remizov was after me because of the botched hit on Ivan. But that's not it at all. He's pissed that I stole his files.

"What's this flash drive?" Ivan asks me.

"Hang on," I say to him. "I'll explain after."

I turn back to Zima.

"Who hired me to kill Ivan?"

Zima searches through his files once more and pulls up a fresh dossier.

"This guy," he says, pointing one long, skinny finger at the screen.

I see an old man with thinning hair and a suit that doesn't fit on the shoulders.

"Who the fuck is Lyosha Egorov?" I say in bewilderment.

I've never seen this guy in my life. But Ivan seems to recognize him.

He's almost . . . blushing?

"He's the husband of a woman I used to . . . date," Ivan admits.

I can't help letting out a snort of laughter.

"Are you serious?"

"Yes," Ivan says.

"That was a big contract," I say. "That chick must have been really hot. Because her husband is *pissed* at you."

"How much was the contract?" Ivan asks curiously.

"Five hundred K."

He nods, eyebrows raised. "That probably cleared his whole bank account," he says.

I want to point out the incredible irony that after all the things Ivan's done, all the people's he's pissed off, the thing that almost got him killed was messing around with a married woman.

But I can tell he's already embarrassed, so I keep a lid on it for the moment.

"What's on that drive?" I ask Zima.

"I don't know!" he says. And then, seeing the look of disbelief on Ivan's face, "I really don't!"

"Well," I say, "you're going to figure it out."

Zima is ten times the hacker I am. I couldn't crack the encryption on the drive, but I bet he can.

"Get your laptop," I tell him. "You're coming with us."

## 18

### IVAN

I'm driving back to Sloane's old apartment. She says the flash drive is hidden there, and that it might still be readable.

I'm not thinking about the flash drive, though. I'm thinking about Lyosha Egorov.

For once in my life, I actually feel guilty.

Nadia Egorov meant nothing to me, but she must have meant something to Lyosha. He risked everything to take revenge on me.

It would have confounded me before. Now I understand a little better how a woman can drive a man mad.

What would I do if I married Sloane, and then lost her to someone else?

I can't even imagine it.

Sloane knows what's bothering me. She's ignoring Zima, who's trussed up in the back of the van. She's watching my face instead.

"What are you going to do to him?" she asks me.

"To Egorov?"

"Yeah."

"I don't know," I say.

Before, I would have ordered him cut into a thousand pieces and the pieces fed to my dogs.

But now, I feel like he was only doing what any man would have to do. If he really loved his woman.

"I was thinking you should send him a fruit basket," Sloane says innocently. "After all, if he hadn't hired me to kill you, we never would have met."

I can't help laughing. I've tried a hundred times to tame this woman, but she has this rowdiness inside of her that can never be extinguished.

"That's not a bad idea," I say. "You can help me pick it out."

We pull up in front of Sloane's flat. The top floor is a smoking ruin, the whole apartment complex taped off. Leaving Zima tied up in the van, Sloane and I scale the iron fire escape up the side of the building.

The metal stairs creak and sway the higher up we get. The staircase is barely connected to the bricks up at the top because of the hole that's been blown in the wall.

I have to boost Sloane the last five or six feet up to the fourth floor. She helps pull me up after her.

Then we're standing in her kitchen, or what's left of it. A few items remain miraculously untouched: a single porcelain mug up on a distant shelf. A magazine thrown to the far corner of the room, only singed a bit on one corner.

The rest of the kitchen looks like a war zone. Shattered dishes, torn-up flooring, the twisted remains of the stove.

It gives me a sick feeling, knowing that Sloane was here when it happened.

"Don't worry," she says, laying her hand on my forearm. "It was a pretty shitty apartment even before the grenade."

"I can see why you preferred the cell," I reply.

As we pick our way around the massive hole in the floor, Sloane leads me into her living room.

Here, too, most everything has been burned up or blown to pieces, though this room was farthest from the blast. Sloane heads straight back to the white brick fireplace, which is mostly in one piece.

She pulls out one of the bricks from the left-hand side of the mantle. In the gap behind the brick sits a little metal box.

"Fireproof," Sloane says with satisfaction.

She tucks the box in her pocket, and we head out of the apartment once more, this time though the front door.

"Remizov must have a copy of whatever's on there," I tell Sloane.

"Oh yeah? What makes you say that?"

"Because he didn't care if it got blown up in your apartment."

Sloane nods, seeing the logic in that.

"Probably," she agrees. "But that doesn't mean it's not valuable."

Once we get back to the van, I drive us a few blocks away to a more deserted part of town, while Sloane pulls the tape off Zima's mouth. I noticed he didn't even try to wriggle out of his bonds while we were gone. He's lying in the exact same position and seems entirely resigned to being a captive.

Once he can speak again, he says, "Can we stop at Teremok or something? I haven't had any breakfast yet."

"It's ten o'clock at night," Sloane says.

"I'm a night owl," Zima says with a shrug.

I can tell Sloane is debating how best to motivate Zima. In the end, she decides on the carrot over the stick.

"I'll get you some food," she agrees. "But first I want you to decode this drive."

"I can't work on an empty stomach," Zima whines.

"Can you work with a broken ankle?" I growl from the front seat.

Sloane holds up her hand to me.

"Flash drive first, then food," she says to Zima firmly.

Zima groans and rolls over so he can squirm himself up into a sitting position.

"Fine," he says. "But I'll need my hands."

Sloane cuts his bonds. He makes a big show of rubbing his wrists, which are barely red. Then he sits cross-legged, opens the laptop on his lap, and inserts the flash drive.

Once he's got it in place, his eyes gleam with interest.

"This is a tricky little system," he says happily.

"Can you figure it out?" Sloane asks.

"I dunno. Probably."

He starts typing away, his expression bright and focused for the first time since we met him. It's quite the transformation. While before I was wondering if we even had the right person, now I can see the intelligence in this kid. The genius, even.

"What are you doing brokering hits?" I ask him. "A kid with your talent."

Zima gives me a look of disgust. "What, are you going to tell me to get a real job?" he says. "Bit hypocritical coming from you two."

"No," I say. "Maybe just something that won't get you killed. Once Remizov realizes you're not getting the flash drive for him . . ."

"Yeah, I know," Zima says. "I won't go back to that apartment. I've got others."

"Do you clean the other ones?" Sloane says.

"Not much," Zima admits.

"Where're your parents?" I press him. I should let it go, but I don't want this kid getting killed the minute we drop him off. Maybe because he reminds me of Karol a little.

"I'm adopted," Zima says, still typing away furiously. "Bit of a cuckoo situation. I outgrew the nest by the time I was twelve years old. My parents are a janitor and a grocery-store clerk. Nice people, but they didn't know what to do with me."

I take a sharp left at the next intersection.

I'm not just going to dump Zima off in the middle of nowhere.

"Where are you going?" Sloane asks me.

"I'll take him back to the compound," I tell her. "He can stay there awhile."

Sloane cocks her head, giving me an appraising look.

I don't know if my sympathy for this kid will earn me any points in her eyes—Sloane is no softy herself. But she seems to respect my decision.

When we're about five minutes away from the monastery, Zima stops typing. He looks up at us.

"Got it," he says.

"Really?" Sloane asks, grabbing the laptop.

"Yeah," Zima says, in his offhand way. He doesn't seem any more animated by success than he was by our threats. The only thing that seems to get this kid excited is a challenge.

Sloane scrolls through the files, her face slack with aston-ishment.

"What is it?" I ask her.

"It's . . . everything," she says. "All Remizov's dirt on everybody. Offshore accounts, details of dirty business deals, pictures of mistresses, criminal evidence. He's got half the bosses in St. Petersburg by the balls."

"Not anymore," I say. "Now we've got them instead."

"I guess so . . ." Sloane says.

She's still scrolling through the files, her face growing increasingly pale.

"What is it?" I ask her.

"It's just . . . there's some dark shit in here," she says.

She turns the screen so I can see.

It's true.

Some of the evidence involves crimes that even I would consider beyond the pale. For instance, it appears that the governor made his money in a chemical plant that's been leeching chemicals into the soil of a nearby town, causing cancer rates to skyrocket. And the commissioner seems to have a penchant for underage girls.

It's no wonder they're at Remizov's beck and call.

He's blackmailing them.

"Who did you get this drive from?" I ask Sloane.

"From Yozhin, the Minister of the Admiralteysky District. Remizov brought it to him at the club. Yozhin was supposed to deliver it to someone else. But I killed him first."

She pauses, glancing over at Zima.

"Who hired me to kill Yozhin?" she asks him.

"That was Boyko Honchar," Zima says, promptly. When Sloane and I look at each other blankly, Zima says, "He's run against Yozhin three times for Admiralteysky. Guess he didn't want to lose a fourth time."

"So Yozhin was killed for a petty political rivalry," Sloane says, thinking out loud. "And I stole the flash drive, which was probably supposed to go to the governor or some other politician. As proof of what Remizov has over them."

"Remizov figured out that you took it," I say. "He probably has his own copy. So, to keep his leverage, he has to get the drive back. Or kill us. Or both."

"Unless we get him first," Sloane says.

We've pulled up to the compound once more.

I let Zima out, with instructions to Andrei to feed him, keep an eye on him, and not let him near any computers.

Back in the van with Sloane, we sit quietly for a moment, both thinking.

I know that neither of us likes what we saw on that drive. The idea of using that information for our own blackmail campaign is hardly appetizing.

Besides, blackmail becomes less effective with the more people that have the information. If Remizov and I both try to twist the governor's arm in opposite directions, using the same leverage, we'll essentially cancel each other out.

There's another way to use the flash drive. One that sticks the knife in Remizov instead. And doesn't turn my stomach quite so much . . .

"What are you thinking?" Sloane says to me, her face as troubled as my own. "What do you want to do with the drive?"

"I think we should give it away," I tell her.

## 19

## SLOANE

I find myself traveling to Moscow after all, via the Sapsan train. It only takes about four hours, but I book a sleeper compartment so I can get a little rest on the journey. It's twenty-five hundred rubles for first class—less than forty dollars American.

I lie in the bunk, too keyed up to actually sleep despite the soothing rocking motion of the train.

I don't disagree with Ivan's plan. But I'm suspicious of his insistence that I have to deliver the flash drive by hand. I'm wondering if he's just trying to get me out of St. Petersburg.

He knows the release of this information will be explosive. I think he's afraid that I'll be caught up in the wave of retaliation that follows.

I don't want to be treated as fragile. I like Ivan because he sees me as an equal. A partner. I don't want him to try to manipulate me, to send me away for my own safety.

I do agree, at least, with his choice of the *Novoya Gazeta* as the best place to hand over the flash drive.

It's not easy to find independent journalists in Russia. The government has taken control of most major newspapers and radio stations, as well as all national television channels. Most media is pure propaganda.

But that doesn't mean there are no critical voices left. Some real journalists remain. And they pay dearly for speaking the truth. Fifty-eight have been murdered in the last thirty years. The investigation into their deaths is a joke.

The very few independent papers dig into the corruption of politicians, business, and banks in Russia, and publish the results.

The *Novoya Gazeta* is one such paper. They themselves have lost six journalists after publishing stories on money laundering, embezzlement, and fraud amongst Russia's elite. Their journalists have been poisoned, shot, and beaten to death with a hammer on the doorstep of their own apartment building. And still, they recently published a story about the kidnapping and murder of immigrant women by Russian police.

So this is where Ivan has sent me. To the offices of *Novoya Gazeta,* to speak with Editor-in-Chief Alya Morozova.

I arrive before their office opens, purchasing a coffee from a little cafe across the street while I wait for Alya to arrive.

I've already looked up her picture online, so I'll know how to recognize her.

Old habits die hard. I can't help researching people before I meet them. I know, for instance, that Alya's sister was one of the six journalists killed, after writing a story about the lynching of Chechens by Russian military. I know that Alya has since published several more stories about the persecution of gay men in Chechnya. She's stubborn. Vengeful. Unbreakable.

She's a tall, slim woman, about forty-five, with iron-gray hair and horn-rimmed glasses. She's wearing an elegant coat and high-heeled boots when she strides up the sidewalk toward her office.

I make sure to approach her head-on—I'm sure she's wary of people sneaking up behind her.

"*Dobroye utro,*" I greet her. *Good morning.*

She takes one look at me and says, "You're not Russian. Do you prefer to speak in English?"

I'm a little taken aback. It's uncomfortable to be sized up so easily. But I always appreciate bluntness.

"Sure," I say. "That works."

"What do you want?" Alya asks, peering at me through her glasses.

Russians also like bluntness. They treat everything as if it costs money, including the number of words in their sentences.

"I have some information for you," I tell her. "Can we go up to your office?"

She looks suspicious, but since that's where she was headed anyway, she makes no objection. She unlocks the front door of the building, and I follow her inside.

The *Gazeta* offices are far from luxurious. Independent journalism is no lucrative affair, despite all the awards the *Gazeta* has won. I know they've been sued multiple times, and often lost. The courts are no fairer than any other institution in Russia.

Alya's desk is just one of many on an open floor plan, not separated in any way. She heads over to the little kitchenette to make her own coffee, and then meets me back at her desk. She takes a tin of shortbread cookies out of her desk, not offering me any.

"So what do you have for me?" she says.

I hand over the flash drive, free for anyone to read now, thanks to Zima.

Alya plugs it into her laptop and begins scrolling. I see her face grow increasingly amazed, the farther down she reads.

She takes off her glasses and presses her thumb and index fingers into the inner corners of her eyes.

She looks more pained than excited.

"Where did you get this?" she asks me.

"I stole it off a politician in a strip club," I tell her.

There's no reason to lie. I'm guessing that Alya is probably as good at sussing out bullshit as Ivan himself.

"Do you have additional sources?" she says.

"No. Most of the evidence speaks for itself, though."

She's watching me through narrowed eyes. Her gaze is no less intimidating without the glasses. I suspect they're just for show, because she seems to see just fine without them.

"Why did you bring this to me?" she snaps. "What are you trying to get out of it?"

"Well, I don't like some of the stuff in there," I tell her.

That's true enough. Some of it turns my stomach. I hate the idea of keeping it secret, using it for leverage myself. I was relieved when Ivan came up with this idea instead.

But Alya knows there's more to it than that.

"Who are you trying to get into trouble?" she persists. "Which of these people?"

"None of them," I tell her. "I don't even know them."

That's sort of true. I don't personally know anybody mentioned on the flash drive.

Alya is folding and unfolding her glasses, debating with herself. She knows all of this is highly suspicious. But of course, she wants the drive.

"Who are you?" she says. "What are you doing in Russia?"

"Amanda Wallace," I say, giving her my name from the strip club. "I was working at a club called Raketa. That's where I got the drive."

She purses her lips. She doesn't believe I'm a stripper.

"What do you want in exchange for the drive?" she asks.

It'll look even sketchier if I don't ask for anything. So I say, "Five hundred dollars."

"I'll give you two hundred."

"Three fifty. I had to take the train from St. Petersburg."

"Two fifty," she says.

"Fine," I say. "But I want those cookies, too."

I nod toward the little tin of shortbread cookies.

Alya snorts and shoves the tin toward me.

"My grandmother made those," she tells me. "They're shit."

I take one out of the tin anyway and dunk it in my coffee while Alya counts the money out of petty cash. She gives it to me partly in American bills, partly in Rubles, because that's what she's got on hand.

I don't make a fuss about it. I just fold up the bills and shove them in my pocket.

"You going to tell me what your real angle is on this?" Alya says, looking up at me while I stand up from my seat.

"It's not relevant," I tell her.

She purses her lips and scowls, putting her glasses back on her face once more. She starts typing on her laptop, dismissing me.

She hasn't thanked me for the flash drive, but I know she's going to use it, nonetheless.

As I'm about to leave she says, without looking up, "You going to take those cookies?"

"No," I say. "You're right—they're shit."

She snorts and puts the tin back in her drawer.

# 20

# IVAN

Sloane texts me from Moscow to let me know that the *Gazeta* has accepted the flash drive. I'm sure it will take them a few days to comb through the files, do their fact-checking and substantiating research, and run everything by their legal department. Maybe a few weeks even. But soon enough, stories are going to start coming out, targeting every single ally Remizov has blackmailed into cooperation.

And then an almighty hellfire is going to rain down on his head.

Every powerful friend he has in St. Petersburg is going to turn into a bitter enemy.

And I'll just be sitting on the sidelines, laughing with glee.

It's not the usual way I do things. I've never shot somebody with an information bullet before. But I have to admit, it feels pretty satisfying all the same.

After all, Remizov hasn't been a typical adversary. He's forced me to get a little more creative.

The only downside is the waiting.

I'd love to call him up and laugh in his face right now.

It's no good tipping him off, though. I'll just have to be patient.

I'm not at all patient while waiting for Sloane at the train station. I tried to convince her to stay in Moscow until after the stories come out, but she wouldn't listen to me. She's so goddamned stubborn.

"I'm not a delicate little flower, Ivan," she laughed, over the phone. "Remizov might just as well be afraid of me."

"I know how capable you are," I told her, trying not to let my anxiety come through in my voice. "But there's a difference between staying under the radar and being right in the crosshairs."

"I know that," Sloane snapped.

"If you just stayed in Moscow a few weeks until everything blows over . . ."

"If you don't want me at your place, that's fine," Sloane said coldly. "But I'm not hiding out here. I'm coming back to St. Petersburg."

"I do want you at my place," I told her quickly. "I absolutely want that. I'll come get you at the train station."

"You don't have to. I can just—"

"I'm coming," I told her, firmly. "I'll be waiting to pick you up."

"Fine," she said, the note of annoyance still in her voice.

Now I'm waiting here for her, having arrived almost a half hour before her train is due, and I'm practically tearing my hair out, wishing her phone had service on the train so I could check in with her.

It's true what I said to Sloane—I know that if anybody can take care of themselves, it's her. But the idea of anything happening to her terrifies me.

I didn't think I wanted a woman in my life.

But I absolutely want *this* woman.

I want Sloane, and nobody else.

She came into my life unbidden, unwanted.

She got into my head, under my skin, until I could hardly think about anything else.

When I thought she'd left for good, I was so . . . blank. The idea that she might vanish as abruptly as she'd appeared was intolerable. It made me realize how dull and cold my life had been before I met her. I didn't want to go back to that.

And then she showed up in my driveway once more, and I couldn't deny how happy I was to see her.

Excitement. Happiness. Connection . . . Love. These are things I didn't expect or want to feel.

Actually, they fucking terrify me.

Putting your emotions into another person is dangerous.

If I care about Sloane, it's like I've cut off a part of myself and put it inside of her. And if she decides to leave again, or if something happens to her . . . that piece of me is just gone. Lost or destroyed.

It's a risk.

A risk I shouldn't take.

But I'm not sure I have a choice.

I care about her. It happened without any decision or consent.

And I'm afraid it's only going to get stronger. The more time I spend with Sloane, the more I want.

To distract myself, I call my brother to check in.

"Hey," Dom says, sounding slightly out of breath.

"What are you doing?"

"Playing Call of Duty."

"With the kid?"

"Yeah."

"How's he doing?"

"He's fucking smoking us," Dom says sourly.

Zima has been settling in at the compound surprisingly well. He seems to like the company and the evening-centric schedule. I had only planned to let him stay a few days, to make sure he didn't suffer the blowback for the loss of the flash drive. But now I'm thinking he might be useful. Unasked, he fixed a bug in the security cameras, and gave Dom some good advice on the perimeter sensors.

We don't exactly have a tech guy, and Zima is a veritable savant.

Granted, the kid eats more than my three biggest guys. But with skills like his, I'd at least break even.

"You get Sloane yet?" Dom asks.

"Just waiting."

"You bring anybody with you?"

"No."

I want to be alone with Sloane. I'm planning to take her out for dinner, once her train comes in. We've never been on an actual date. I'd love to see her sitting across from me at a candlelit table.

"None of us should go out alone," Dom says. "Not 'till all this shit with Remizov is settled."

I know he's just thinking about Karol. But it irritates me when my little brother tries to lay down the law. Especially when I know he's right.

"I won't be alone once I pick her up," I tell Dom, a note of warning in my voice. "Worry about yourself and the rest of the men."

"Everything's good here," Dom says, unoffended. "I've got three people patrolling. Everyone's on alert."

The train pulls into the station at last.

I hear it before I see it, and then I see it rushing in, pulling cleanly to a stop, and opening up the doors to allow the passengers to stream out.

"Gotta go," I say to Dom, "she's here."

But I haven't actually seen Sloane on the platform yet.

I get out of the car, walk up the steps to the open platform to look for her.

Tourists and commuters pass me by on both sides, the stream parting around the immovable rock. I scan each of them, as if I wouldn't recognize Sloane's slim figure and lovely face immediately.

I can already feel the sick, rushing dread in the pit of my stomach, though I'm telling myself it's too soon to worry, she was probably just at the back of the train, or she's stopped at the bathrooms, or I just missed her in the crowd.

But the platform is clearing, and she's nowhere to be seen.

I pull my phone out of my pocket, my fingers so numb that I almost drop it on the cement.

I check for a message or a missed call from Sloane.

For a moment I wonder if she decided to stay in Moscow after all, but of course that's stupid. She was adamantly against that idea, and she would have told me if she changed her mind. She knew I was coming to the station to pick her up.

A deeper part of my brain worries that she decided to go somewhere else entirely. She could have a flat in Paris, in Tokyo, in Madagascar for all I know. She might even have gone back to America.

But I don't think that's it, either.

The other alternative I don't even want to consider.

I hit her number, the phone seeming to take forever to connect.

It rings and rings.

There's no answer from Sloane.

I hang up and try again.

Ringing and ringing, without any response.

Sloane doesn't have voicemail.

I assume she switches phone numbers every month or two, the same as I do.

My mind is racing.

How can I find out if she bought a ticket? If she boarded the train?

I feel like I should get on before it leaves again—try to find a conductor, ask if anyone saw her.

But maybe I should stay here at the station where we were supposed to meet?

I've never been so indecisive before.

I'm a fucking mess, this isn't like me at all.

I always know what to do. I always have a plan.

My phone buzzes in my hand, like an insect trapped in my palm.

It's so startling that I almost drop it again.

I see an unknown number on the screen.

And I already know what I'll hear when I pick up.

But all I can do is answer.

I hit the icon. Hold the phone to my ear, listening silently.

"Your girlfriend is very pretty," the cold voice says.

My hand is shaking. My whole body is trembling with rage.

"Where is she?" I say.

Each word comes out through lips frozen with fury and fear. I can hardly understand myself. But Remizov understands perfectly.

"She's my guest," he says.

I want to scream at Remizov that if he hurts her, if he so much as touches her, I won't rest until everything he's ever known or loved is a smoking ruin.

But that would be the stupidest thing of all. He can't know how I feel about Sloane. That would be signing her death warrant.

"What do you want?" I ask.

"I want the flash drive," he says.

He grabbed Sloane, whether from Moscow, or from the train. But he doesn't know why she was there. He doesn't know that we don't have the drive anymore. He thinks I kept it.

He wants to trade it for Sloane. Though of course, it won't be a trade at all. Once he has what he wants, he'll kill us both.

"Bring it to my house," Remizov says, his voice soft and quiet. "I assume you got the address from Zima."

I grunt.

"Come alone," Remizov says. "I don't need to tell you what will happen otherwise."

My teeth are grinding together so hard it feels like my molars are going to crack. The urge to shout at Remizov, to threaten him, is almost overwhelming.

"I'll get the drive," I say. "And I'll be there in an hour."

# 21

# SLOANE

*'Tis best to weigh the enemy more mighty than he seems.*

— SHAKESPEARE

fter I meet with Alya at the *Gazeta* offices, I've got some time to kill. I booked tickets on the afternoon train back to St. Petersburg, leaving at 4:00 p.m.

I spend some of that time fighting with Ivan, who wants me to hide out here while he slugs it out with Remizov. Obviously, that's not happening. We agreed to work together on this little project—I'm not going to be a glorified UPS delivery guy.

It's sweet that Ivan's worried about me.

But I don't want him to be worried about me. I want him to trust me.

Which is what makes it so extraordinarily irritating when I see three men watching me on the train.

It's hard for thugs and mercenaries to blend in. How often do you see two or three men together who are all over six feet tall, bursting out of their jackets, and sporting military-style haircuts?

They can sit apart from each other on the train, they can try to act casual. One of them is even pretending to read a Russian magazine. But even there, he hasn't got the rhythm quite right. He's turning the pages too regularly, not skipping the boring articles and spending a long time on the stuff that interests him.

And, invariably, they keep glancing in my direction. Not often, and not all at the same time. But with enough regularity that I know they're watching me.

At first, I think that Ivan must have sent them to keep tabs on me on the way home.

But I've seen enough of his men to have a pretty good idea what they look like. They're all Russian by birth, and since most of them are related to Ivan in one way or another, there's a certain family resemblance.

These three aren't brothers or cousins. At least one of them looks Armenian, the other Polish or Ukrainian. The third one, the biggest of the lot, just looks plain mean. He might have been good-looking once upon a time, in a college football-player kind of way. But now his face is set in the sort of cruel, calloused lines that show that this guy has done some shit in the years between twenty and thirty-eight. No one wanted to sit in the seats directly around him. Which gives him a clear view right over to me.

I could get up, pretend to go to the toilets and try to switch cars, but I don't want to isolate myself off by the bathrooms or between cars. For the moment I'm safest right here, amongst the muddle of businesspeople and students and tourists. All these witnesses.

I'm assuming these goons plan to grab me when we get off at St. Petersburg.

The train makes several stops before the Moskovskiy station. The closest to St. Petersburg is at Tosno. If I wanted to be really tricky, I'd get off sooner—I know the men will be more vigilant the closer we get to our destination. But I don't want to be stranded in the middle of nowhere.

I try not to look at the three men at all. I make conversation with my seatmate, a woman on her way to visit her sister in St. Petersburg. And I only allow myself to watch the soldiers out of my peripheral view, when I pretend to stretch or glance out the opposite window.

At each stop along our route, I seem to pay no attention as the doors open to allow passengers off and on to the train. But I'm timing the seconds between the warning chimes, and the moment when the doors seal themselves, so the train can take off down the track at 155 miles per hour.

The Tosno station is small. When the doors crack open, only two people from my car get off, and only one old woman gets on. She's carrying an old shopping bag full of books and snacks for the short journey remaining to St. Petersburg.

I wait and wait, pretending to read on my phone, not even glancing up at the doors. The warning bells chime. I stay in my seat as the agonizing seconds tick by.

Right then, the handle of the old woman's shopping bag snaps. Two oranges tumble out of the bag, rolling down the aisle of the train.

I hear the doors chuff as they ready themselves to close.

The man closest to me, the mean-looking one, is distracted by the oranges.

I leap out of my seat and sprint for the doors.

They're already starting to close.

I can hear the three goons behind me, jumping out of their seats, shoving past passengers to chase after me.

They won't make it before the doors close. I'm barely going to make it.

I jump down the steps, the doors sealing themselves behind me, trapping the Armenian and the Ukrainian inside the train.

But the football player has that ungodly speed of a forty-yard rusher, despite his size. And he's smarter than the other two. He didn't chase after me to the same door—he ran to the back of the train. The back doors try to close but he's turned himself sideways and wedged his chest and shoulders through.

The doors make an outraged warning sound. He pries them apart with his beefy arms and keeps forcing himself through the gap, like a grotesque version of birth.

I don't wait around to see if he's going to be successful.

I start running down the platform.

Here's the part of my plan that isn't very smart at all.

Moskovskiy station is large and busy—I might have been able to lose myself in the crowd. And Ivan is waiting for me there.

Tosno station is deserted. The two passengers who disembarked have already disappeared. There isn't an employee or a police officer to be seen. Even the tickets are sold from automatic machines.

I'm running down the open platform, my boots ringing against the cement. I can hear another set of footsteps behind me, much heavier and faster than my own.

I don't even want to look back to see how close the linebacker is getting. I just race down the steps, out to the open parking lot behind the station.

And here's where fate ceases to be my friend.

The platform was shoveled and salted, but the parking lot is full of snow. It's thick and soft. My feet sink down into it. It's like trying to run through sand, but much more slippery.

The linebacker is gaining on me. I can hear his hoarse breath, chugging closer and closer. I try to sprint faster, but I'm tiring out, I can't get purchase. It's like a nightmare where a monster is chasing me, and my legs are getting heavier and heavier.

There's only two or three cars in the lot, no people around. Pointless to scream for help.

No time to get out my phone, to try to call Ivan.

The linebacker tackles me, and my head strikes the ground.

WHEN I WAKE, I'm lying on a soft bed in a cool, dark room.

For a moment, I think that Ivan must have been waiting at the Tosno station. He dealt with the linebacker and brought me back to the monastery.

However, as soon as I sit up, that illusion is dispelled.

This is no monastery.

It's a house, modern in the extreme.

I'm sitting on a platform bed, in a dim and highly luxurious room, decorated in shades of gray and blue. Several architectural prints hang on the walls, and a sleek chandelier dangles from the ceiling.

Yet I notice at once that this room has no windows, not a single one. The drapes hang across blank walls. Along with the digital panel on the wall that controls the light and temperature, I'm quite sure this room is rigged to record video and sound.

I'm in a cell again. Not as obvious as the ones in Ivan's catacombs. But a cell nonetheless.

My head is throbbing, particularly the spot on the left temple, just above the hairline, where my skull struck the snowy ground.

I'm lucky the snow was so thick. If the parking lot had been bare cement, that idiotic goon might have brained me. When apparently his instructions were to bring me back here.

Raising my hand to gingerly touch the lump on my head, I feel a strange jingling on my wrist. I look at my arm and see that I'm wearing a diamond tennis bracelet.

Glancing down at my body, I discover that the simple slacks and blouse I wore to meet with Alya have been replaced with a ball gown. Deep burgundy in color, off the shoulder, with a sweetheart neckline and a slit up the thigh, cascading down into tiers of ruffles.

Someone has put a bracelet on my wrist, earrings in my ears, and shoes on my feet. They've re-dressed me, all the way down to my underwear.

What. The. Fuck.

I swing my legs off the side of the bed and stand up.

Doing so sends a spike of pain shooting through my skull. A wave of nausea washes over my body, making me sway so I almost have to sit down again. I'm unsteady on my feet, especially in these ridiculous shoes. I hate high heels with a passion. I agree with the feminist who said that men invented high heels so women couldn't run away from them.

In point of fact, the dress and the shoes are hobbling me, and weighing me down. I'm tempted to strip them all off again. I'd rather be naked, like I was at Ivan's house. That was more honest, as well as more practical.

But I'm quite sure that Remizov is watching me. And I'm not sure I want to start antagonizing him. At least, not yet.

I do intend to go find him, however.

He didn't bring me here and dress me like this for no reason.

He wants to use me as some kind of bait or pawn against Ivan.

Well, if that's his plan, we might as well get on with it.

Sure enough, when I stride over to the door and try to turn the handle, it swings open.

I make my way down the hallway, descending the stairs to the main level. There I find the linebacker waiting for me, along with the Armenian. They're standing outside a set of double doors, like bouncers outside a nightclub.

The linebacker smirks at me. I'd like to smack him right in his smug face for this lump he gave me. His eyes are crawling over my body in the revealing dress. He better not have been the one who changed my clothes.

"Next time, run faster," he grunts at me. He gives me a wicked grin, showing off his straight, white teeth.

"Next time, try not to dress like an extra in *Die Hard* so I don't spot you five minutes out of Moscow," I tell him.

His smile falls off his face and he narrows his eyes at me. His fist tightens. I know he wants to hit me just as much as I want to do the same to him.

But that's not his orders. Not yet, at least.

So instead, he just glares at me while he cracks the door to the adjoining room.

I sweep past him, into the formal dining room.

There I find Remizov himself, sitting alone, eating his dinner.

He's wearing a glossy navy dinner jacket and tie. His hair is combed back. Soft music is playing.

And yet, I can't shake a feeling of deep revulsion as I approach the table.

There's something extremely off-putting about Remizov. It extends from his person to his house. It's all clean, elegant, orderly. But it's also . . . blank. His house is like a hotel. Lacking any elements of personality or experience. And that's how he is in person as well. Watching him cut his steak and take a bite is like watching an android. He chews and swallows, but he hardly seems to taste it.

He looks up at me. Holds out a thin, pale hand.

"Would you like to join me?" he says, in his soft voice.

I sit down opposite Remizov at the long, rectangular table.

There's a plate of steak, mashed potatoes, and asparagus in front of him. A covered platter in front of my own seat. Remizov is sipping from a glass of deep red wine—the exact color of my dress. My glass is empty.

"Go ahead," Remizov says, nodding toward the platter.

I lift the lid, seeing the same well-arranged meal that Remizov is currently eating.

I'm not inclined to partake. I've poisoned too many people to accept a meal from a known enemy.

Remizov chuckles softly, guessing at the reason for my hesitation.

"You're perfectly safe with me, Sloane," he says. "While we wait for your lover to arrive."

I don't know what kind of weird Hannibal Lecter game he's trying to play with me, but I always prefer to be blunt. Especially when I'm scared. And the idea of Ivan showing up here, walking right into Remizov's trap, fucking terrifies me.

"What's your beef with him?" I demand, forcing myself to look Remizov right in his stiff, expressionless face.

"I don't have any 'beef' with Ivan Petrov," Remizov says calmly. He blinks slowly with his strange, faded eyes. "I'm taking over St. Petersburg. I analyzed the major players in the city. I attacked those who were weakest first. Then I worked my way up the list. When it was Ivan's turn, I targeted his weak points. Distracted him while I made alliances. Planned the final blow against him. But then you arrived to . . . complicate the situation."

"No plan survives contact with the enemy," I say.

That was another favorite quote of my father's.

Remizov frowns. He doesn't like me impugning his planning abilities.

"Interesting that you position yourself as my enemy," he says. "You and I have no conflict. Other than the matter of my flash drive."

"And the fact that you blew up my apartment," I say, "and tried to kill me."

"Simply an attempt to retrieve my property," he says. "Or neutralize it. Nothing personal."

I laugh, remembering that I once said the same thing to Ivan.

Remizov doesn't like that laugh either. He doesn't understand the joke, and I can tell that when he doesn't understand something, it angers him.

"You're not a Petrov," he says sharply. "I read your file from Zima's computer. You're an American. Your father was CIA."

"What's your point?"

"You have no loyalty to Ivan Petrov. You were hired to kill him, and you failed to complete the job. Why are you working with him now? Why didn't you leave, after you lost your apartment?"

I shrug, not wanting to give Remizov any more information than he already has.

"I like St. Petersburg," I say.

To stay on the conversational offensive, I add, "Why are you so determined to take over? You're not Bratva either."

"That's right," Remizov says. He takes another bite of his steak, chewing slowly, and washing it down with a swallow of wine. "I have no family. No clan. That's a strength, not a weakness. My organization will be a true meritocracy. Not weighed down by tradition and birthright."

He looks me over, in the revealing red dress.

It takes a lot to make me uncomfortable, but his cold, inhuman stare does it. He's not like a normal man, inflamed by lust. He evaluates me the same way he probably evaluated the furniture for this house. With no attachment or emotion—just a consideration of whether or not it would fit his purposes.

"You Americans appreciate egalitarianism," he says. "With the exception of the contract on Petrov, you're good at your job. Ivan isn't leaving this house tonight—he had his chance to fall in line, and he refused. But I extend the same offer to you that I did to him. Come work for me. I'm always in need of good help."

Men are always offering to hire me. As if I've just been wandering around, pining for a good healthcare plan and a

401K. Usually it annoys me. But the only part of that paragraph I can seem to focus on is "Ivan isn't leaving this house tonight."

Remizov intends to kill him.

I can't let that happen.

If Ivan comes here, it will be for my sake.

If he takes that risk for me, I can't let him die.

"So," Remizov says, putting down his fork. "Where is it? Where is the drive? I assume you took it to Moscow with you?"

It takes every ounce of my self-control not to stare at him with my mouth hanging open.

He doesn't know what I was doing in Moscow.

He knows I went there. His men found me on the train back. But they missed my meeting first thing in the morning.

"Ivan has it," I lie smoothly. "My trip to Moscow had nothing to do with the drive."

Remizov stares at me, silently. Watching my face.

The tension stretches between us like a rubber band, longer and longer until one of us has to snap.

*He who speaks first, loses.*

It's the oldest trick, and the hardest to withstand. The temptation to fill the silence is almost overwhelming. My father always told me to pinch the skin on the inside of my palm to relieve the anxiety, to help me stay quiet.

I pinch myself hard.

At last, Remizov says, "You know what's on the drive?"

This is a ploy to check my honesty. He's asking me a question to which he already knows the answer.

He knows we've decoded the drive. He wants to see if I'll admit it.

"Yes," I say. "I saw it."

"Did you make copies?"

"No."

Long, painful silence again.

"Don't lie to me," Remizov says softly. "There are no second chances with me."

Well, I might as well swing for the fences then.

"Look," I say, "I don't care about a bunch of dirty little secrets. I stole the drive because I thought I could sell it. But if it's going to be more trouble than it's worth, I'm happy to give it back to you."

I try to sound as reasonable as possible. But all the while that I'm speaking, I'm focusing on the steak knife to the right of my plate. It has a heavy wooden handle, a serrated blade, and a sharply pointed tip.

"If you don't mind," I say to Remizov, "I would like some of that wine after all."

"Of course," he says.

He lifts the dark-colored bottle, pours the thick red wine into my glass. While he's doing so, I slip the knife off the table, into my lap.

Then I take the glass and raise it.

"What should we toast to?" I say.

"To new management," Remizov says.

"To new management," I agree.

With my right hand, I hold up my glass. With my left, I clutch the steak knife. As Remizov leans forward to clink his glass against mine, I swing the knife, intending to plunge it into the side of his throat.

Remizov catches my hand, his cold fingers closing around my wrist like a manacle.

He's moved so fast that I can hardly understand what's happened. I've dropped my wineglass. It tips over on the table, the dark liquid spreading across the bare wood. But Remizov hasn't spilled a drop.

He gives a sharp twist to my wrist. My hand opens helplessly, the knife clattering down on the table next to the wine glass.

Remizov shoves me back down in my seat.

My heart is beating so fast it feels like it's on fire.

Remizov hardly even looks angry—just annoyed.

"Consider your offer of employment rescinded," he says. "And don't try that again."

I've never seen someone move so fast.

I have a horrible feeling that after all that's happened, I've still underestimated this man.

Remizov glances down at his watch. It's a Vacheron Constantine. One of the simplest models, with no numbers or complications. Plain and utilitarian, if you can say that about a twenty thousand-dollar watch.

"Ivan said he would be here in an hour," Remizov says. "Do you think he's on his way?"

Ivan could stay home, I suppose. Wait for Remizov to send him another horrific package to his gate. He'll know this is a trap as well as I do. Staying home would be the smart thing to do.

Yet I'm sure that he'll come for me.

I have no reason to believe it.

It defies all sense and reason.

But I know he will.

"He'll come," I tell Remizov.

"I hope, for your sake, that he does," Remizov says.

There's a knock on the door.

The linebacker pokes his head inside.

His face is all politeness when he addresses Remizov—no trace of his hateful smirk.

"He's here," he says.

# 22

# IVAN

I don't take any weapons, not even a knife.

It's pointless, when I know Remizov will have me searched before I get within fifty feet of him.

I do take a flash drive. It's not Remizov's flash drive, of course—that one is still in Moscow. But it looks very similar. Close enough to fool him for a minute, I hope. I slip it into my pocket.

As I'm getting ready to go, my brother knocks on my door.

He knows I was supposed to pick up Sloane at the train station. He saw me arrive back home without her.

Seeing my clothes and the expression on my face, he guesses at once what I'm about to do.

"You can't be serious," Dom says.

"I'm going, and I'm going alone," I tell him.

"Ivan. This is madness."

"It's pointless to talk about it. My mind is made up."

I'm lacing my shoes, avoiding looking at my brother. But I can see him standing in the doorway, his face looking pale next to his blond hair, his arms folded across his chest.

"Is this because of Karol?" he asks.

I look sharply up at him.

"*No,*" I say. "It's not because of Karol. I can't let Remizov hurt Sloane."

"But he *is* going to hurt her," Dom says, his lips white with anger and fear. "He's going to kill her and you as well. This isn't a rescue mission, it's suicide. At the very least, I'm coming with you, and the rest of the—"

"No!" I cut across him. "As soon as we drive up, he'll kill her. He told me to come by myself."

"I'm not going to let you do that," Dom says.

He's definitely blocking the doorway. He's standing with his legs apart, determined not to let me pass.

I stand up so we're eye to eye, not a centimeter's difference between our heights. I've never hit my brother before, outside of training. But I'll hit him now, if he tries to stand in my way.

"I'm still in charge here," I tell him.

"I know you are," Dom says, his blue eyes darker than usual. "I'll follow you anywhere, brother. But I won't let you go to your death alone."

The time is ticking away. I told Remizov I would be at his place in an hour. If it comes down to a fight with Dominik, I think I'll win. But I might seriously hurt him. And I'll be worn out before I even leave, besides being late.

Taking him is not an option. I'm well aware that my chances of returning home again are minuscule. I'll need Dom to take over for me here. He's the only one who can.

So he can't come with me.

It's not happening.

Unless . . .

I'm thinking fast, remembering who else we have in the house right now.

"You can come," I say to my brother. "But just you. And Zima."

"Zima?" Dom says in surprise.

"Go get him," I say. "Ask him if he'll help us with something."

Dom looks at me suspiciously, like he thinks I'm going to try to sneak away while he's retrieving Zima from the TV room.

"I'll wait right here," I promise him.

Dom nods and disappears down the hallway.

Sooner than I dared hope, he returns with Zima slouching along behind him. Zima's light brown hair looks messier than ever, but at least he's been showering since he came here, and we got him some new clothes.

"You need something, boss?" he says.

I know he's only calling me that because everybody else does. His tone is mildly mocking. But I hope he means it too, in his own way.

"You know Remizov's house?" I say to Zima.

"Yeah."

"Do you think you could hack into his system?"

Zima shrugs.

"I could try."

WE DRIVE IN SEPARATE CARS. I tell Dom five times over that he's got to wait at least twenty minutes to even leave the compound, and he's got to drive the long way round. If Remizov's men are watching this place, if they have the slightest clue I'm not coming alone, it will all be for nothing.

Dom agrees, though I can tell he doesn't want to.

He takes Zima with him, and they wait in Dom's GLK while I pull out alone in my Hummer.

As I drive to Remizov's house, I don't feel any fear for myself.

My concern is all for Sloane. I doubt she went quietly when they grabbed her in Moscow. I should have made Remizov put her on the phone, to make sure he hasn't hurt her.

But I don't think that's his way. He won't risk killing either of us until he has the flash drive safe in hand. After that, all bets are off.

It's only about a twenty-minute drive to Krestovsky.

How strange that we've been living so close to each other all this time.

I don't know Remizov at all. We have no relationship, no history, for good or for ill. Yet I hate him more than anyone I've known, for the callous way he murdered Karol, and for his audacity in thinking he can take what belongs to me and the other Bratva of St. Petersburg. What our families have built over two hundred years, he thinks he can claw away from us in the space of a few months.

He thinks we'll make deals with him. Agree to serve under him.

Maybe some of the Bratva have done it, but I never will.

I'd rather be dead than on my knees.

*Would you rather see Sloane dead, though?*

That's a more difficult question.

That's the problem with caring about someone. No logic, no ideals can withstand the imperative of keeping that person safe.

I've only known Sloane a short time, but I do know her. I know exactly who she is, what she's capable of. And I want her to be mine.

I have a vision of the two of us at the head of the Petrov family. Equals and partners. Building an empire that makes Remizov's ambitions look like nothing more than a fever dream.

I can see it so clearly, what Sloane and I could achieve together. So clearly that even though I know I'm supposed to be walking into certain death, I can't believe that what I'm imagining won't come to pass.

After all these years of living in a monastery, I've finally found faith in something.

This girl who tried to kill me, and instead, brought me new life.

I'm almost happy as I pull through the gates to Remizov's house.

Because I'm about to see Sloane again.

I'd rather die next to her than live without her.

I park my car and walk toward the front steps.

In my peripheral view, I see half a dozen guards patrolling the grounds, with several more stationed around the front door. I'm sure Remizov has all hands on deck tonight, in case I disobeyed his order and brought all my men with me.

I hold up my empty hands as I approach the door.

Still, two of his guards search me so thoroughly that I couldn't have smuggled a pencil inside the house.

When they're satisfied that I came unarmed, they lead me inside.

Remizov's house is large and modern, relentlessly masculine in its colors and aesthetic. The rooms are spotlessly clean, smelling of cleaning products and little else.

It seems like he lives here alone, other than his men on their rotating shifts. I wonder if he gets any pleasure out of the vast, opulent rooms, the art on the walls, the cars in his garage, or if he's simply driven by instinct to collect and expand, like a dragon with its hoard.

I could ask him.

His guards lead me to a set of double doors. There's another pair of goons guarding the doors. I immediately dislike the look of the one on the right. He's built like a tank, with short cropped hair and a clean-shaven face. He has a broad jaw, a cleft chin—and a conceited smirk that I want to wipe off his face with my fist.

He makes an exaggerated show of opening the door for me, but then stands in such a way that we knock shoulders as I walk through the opening.

I want to wheel around and throttle him. But I can't spare a second on him or anyone else. I need to see Sloane.

I don't have to wait long.

She's sitting in the dining room across from Remizov himself. As soon as I enter, she leaps to her feet.

She's never looked more beautiful than she does in this moment. She's wearing a deep red gown that shows her long, slender neck, the smooth skin of her shoulders, and the tops of her breasts. Her black curls are wild around her face, trailing down her back. Her eyes are brilliant, full of hope and excitement at the sight of me. She's smiling—despite everything, she's smiling. She calls out my name.

I want to run over to her, touch her face, make sure she's alright. I want to kiss her. But I've already made a mistake, letting Remizov see my pleasure and relief at the sight of her. I meant to stay calm and cold.

He's sitting across the table from Sloane, watching us. He hasn't gotten up as I enter. He's wearing a formal jacket, his hair combed back. The table is set as if they're on a date.

I wanted to take Sloane for dinner tonight. This fucking animal is eating and drinking with her instead. He really does want to take everything from me.

The only thing amiss in this little tableau is the glass toppled over on its side, the wine spilled across the table. Sloane is the furthest thing from clumsy. I scan her once more, to make sure nothing has happened to her yet. I notice that her left wrist is red, with four distinct fingerprints marking the flesh. I feel a spark of rage.

Sloane sees my worry, my anger. She doesn't care what Remizov thinks. She intends to run over to me at once. But quick as a snake, Remizov reaches across the table and grabs her wrist once more.

"You stay with me," he hisses.

He pulls her around the table so we're all standing facing each other on the same side—Remizov with Sloane, and me surrounded by the three goons who have followed me inside, including the one who shoulder-checked me. He's standing closest of all, practically breathing down my neck.

One of the guards has an automatic rifle slung over his shoulder. The other two wear guns at their hips. None of the weapons are drawn and pointed at me yet, but I'm sure it's only a matter of time.

Remizov is standing directly next to Sloane, one hand still gripping her wrist, and the other around her waist. I can see her shudder of revulsion as he puts his arm around her. Remizov doesn't seem to care. In fact, I'm quite sure he likes it.

"Isn't she a beauty?" he says softly. "I dressed her this way to remind you what's at stake, Ivan."

"No reminder needed," I say. "You're not exactly subtle."

"Let's proceed, then," Remizov says, dropping the smile. "Give me the drive."

"Let Sloane go first," I say.

"Don't be ridiculous," Remizov snaps. "You have no leverage. She's not going anywhere. Hand it over now."

I had hoped to stall a little longer. Give Dom and Zima time to catch up to me, and hopefully to work a little magic.

Remizov has about as much patience as he has charm, however.

I take the flash drive out of my pocket.

The smirking guard snatches it out of my hand and carries it over to Remizov.

For a single moment his face is alight with satisfaction, but almost as soon as the drive touches his palm, he throws it down in disgust.

"That is not my flash drive," he says. If I thought his voice was cold before, it's now turned to pure ice.

"Yes, it is," I say stupidly.

I hoped he'd at least check on his computer.

Remizov gives a nod to the smirking guard. He takes his gun from his belt and hits me across the back of the head with the barrel.

The pain is instant and blinding. I sink to my knees. The guard hits me again, right across the jaw, this time with his fist.

I go down hard, my head hitting the floor.

I hear Sloane scream. I assume she tried to run over to me, but Remizov kept hold of her. I hear a scuffle and a sharp slap as he hits her across the face.

That's what keeps me conscious. My rage at the sound of that blow.

I'm back on my feet again, my head throbbing, but my vision swiftly clearing. I can see the mark on Sloane's cheek where Remizov struck her. I would be barreling across the room toward him if I weren't being held in place by the two guards gripping my arms.

"Where's the drive?" Remizov says.

"I thought that was it," I say stupidly. "That's the only one we have."

It's a pathetic lie. Not convincing in the slightest.

Grinning harder than ever, the guard balls up his fist and hits me again, in the face, and then in the stomach. I double over, dropping to my knees once more, trying not to retch. I've been punched plenty of times before, but this guy feels like he's made out of granite. Each blow hits me like a sledgehammer.

"Stop!" Sloane screams.

"We can stop any time you want," Remizov says.

"He doesn't have the drive," Sloane cries.

I try to tell her not to say any more, but I haven't got my breath back yet from the blow to the stomach. I'm still gasping and wheezing.

"Where is it?" Remizov says.

"It's in Moscow," Sloane tells him.

"Where?"

"I gave it away. To a journalist."

There's dead quiet in the room as this information sinks in to everyone present.

"A journalist?" Remizov says.

"Yes," Sloane says. "She's going to publish it all."

For the first time, Remizov looks truly angry. His pale eyes become watery with rage, and his thin lips quiver.

But his voice is still flat as he says, "Then it appears the two of you have no use to me anymore."

He looks over at the smirking guard, surely to give the order to shoot us both.

Before he can open his mouth to speak, the lights go out, and the room is plunged into darkness.

## 23

### SLOANE

When the power is cut, for a split-second, I think that I'm dead. The darkness is so immediate and intense, it's like pulling the plug on my own brain.

But then I realize that I'm still very much alive, and so is everyone else.

Only a quarter of a second has gone by.

No one has moved an inch.

I'm considering if I should try to grab the other knife off the table, to stab Remizov in the dark.

But I also know Ivan is surrounded by three guards. And however skilled of a fighter he may be, those aren't good odds.

So I tear myself out of Remizov's grip and run to the table, but I don't grab the knife. I search for the wine bottle instead, scrabbling blindly until my hand closes around the neck. I turn and throw it in the direction where the three men were standing.

I hear the heavy clunk of the bottle striking someone's skull, and then the heavier thud of a body falling to the floor.

At the same moment that I throw the bottle, I hear Ivan diving at someone's legs, and the mad scuffle that follows, in which I have no idea whatsoever who he's fighting, or who might be winning.

I can't pay any attention to it, because as soon as the bottle leaves my hand, I feel Remizov's fingers seizing me by the hair. He yanks me backward off my feet.

I try to kick and punch and claw at him, but he's dragging me backward, my scalp screaming with pain, and my feet stumbling in those detestable high heels.

Remizov knows this house, with or without light to see by.

He drags me across the dining room, out a separate set of doors, and up the stairs behind them.

The whole house is pitch black. There isn't the slightest sound of a heater or fan. I can still hear the grunting and shouting of the struggle in the dining room.

Before we've gone up more than a couple of steps, I hear three gunshots, muffled by the closed doors.

"Ivan!" I scream.

There's no answer from Ivan, or anyone else.

Remizov is still dragging me up the stairs, one hand wrapped tight in my hair, and the other locked around my wrist. He's abominably strong, despite how slim he is. I'm hampered by the goddamned dress and my throbbing head, which hasn't recovered from being tackled by the linebacker, and was aggravated again by Remizov's slap.

I still intend to fight him, even if it sends both of us tumbling down the steps. Feeling this, Remizov jerks his gun out of his jacket and presses it up against my head.

"Stop struggling," he says, "or I'll blow your brains out on this wall."

I don't think he's the bluffing type.

I stop fighting him.

He keeps hold of my wrist, yanking me up the stairs.

I hear more shots outside the building—bursts of gunfire from several locations on the grounds.

I assume that Ivan's men are storming the house—or at least, a few of them. I don't know who he's brought, though I'm sure Dom is there.

Whether they'll make it inside before Remizov kills me is a different question.

I'm not thinking about myself, though.

I'm hoping, praying—actually praying for the first time in my life—that Ivan was the one who fired the gun in the dining room. Assuming I hit one of the guards with the wine bottle, that left two for Ivan to contend with. They were armed; he wasn't. And he'd already been beaten bloody by that damned linebacker.

Yet I'm looking down the staircase, desperately searching for any sign of him.

Remizov drags me relentlessly upward.

When we get to the top floor of the house, he pulls me through a reading room, out onto the balcony. He stands with his back to the rail, facing the doorway. He holds me in front of him, the gun pressed tight against my side.

And then he waits.

It's obvious that I'm his insurance policy.

He can hear the gunfire as clearly as I can.

He's waiting to see who will prevail—Ivan's men, or his.

If it's the linebacker who walks through that door, he'll probably shoot me and throw me over the railing.

If it's Ivan...

I don't see how that can have a happy ending, either.

I wait, and Remizov waits too, his breath hot against my ear, the barrel of the gun digging into my ribs.

## 24

# IVAN

*The best way to find out if you can trust somebody is to trust them.*

— ERNEST HEMINGWAY

When the lights cut out, I have a split-second advantage, because I'm the only person in the room who was anticipating it.

In a high-tech, modern house like Remizov's, the security system, the lights, the music, and the power all run off a single grid, controlled remotely.

I had no idea if Zima would be able to hack into that system. But it was the only idea I could come up with on short notice.

And of course, I couldn't exactly time when the lights would go out. But I was waiting for it. Hoping for it.

The moment the room plunges into darkness, I dive for the legs of the guard closest to me. He goes down hard, and I scramble for the gun at his waist. Before I can get hold of it, someone grabs my feet from behind, jerking me backward.

At the same moment, I hear a thunk, and the sound of a heavy body dropping next to me. For a second I think the other two guards must have gotten confused and attacked each other, but then I hear Sloane struggling with Remizov across the room, and I realize what actually happened—she threw something at one of the guards.

Instead of taking her chance to run or to attack Remizov, she tried to help me instead. She knew I was outnumbered—she helped shift the odds in my favor.

I kick backward hard against whoever has hold of my legs. I hear a grunt of pain as my heel connects with their face. From the sound of it, I think it's the smirking asshole who shoulder-checked me at the door.

I feel hands grasping at me from the other side, and I start punching and pummeling the first guard I tackled before he can pull his gun from his belt.

The smirking guard jumps on my back, and we're all rolling around in a maelstrom of fist and elbows.

Here, too, I have an unexpected factor in my favor—I can kick and hit and gouge anybody I can get my hands on. But in the darkness, the two guards have no idea who they're striking. They're hitting each other as much as they're getting me, and their confusion and frustration is making them ineffective.

With a roar of rage, the larger of the two, the smirking guard, starts swinging haymakers. His sledgehammer fist connects with his colleague's jaw, and the man collapses on top of me. I feel his gun trapped between our bodies, and I try to wrench it out of his belt while the other guard is scrabbling at my throat, his fingernails clawing at my skin, before he finally gets purchase and starts to choke me.

The limp body of the unconscious guard is pinning me down. The other man, abominably strong, is digging his iron-hard fingers into my neck.

"Now I've got you, you fuck," he grunts, his face so close that I can feel his spit on my face.

My fingers are tugging at the holster, trying to free the handgun trapped beneath the dead weight of the other guard. My head is swimming. If I could see anything, the room would be spinning around.

I yank the gun free at last.

I can't see it, of course, but from the feel of it, I think it's a Glock. Which means there's no safety to release, just a trigger safety.

I put my finger in the correct position, point the gun right at the smirking guard, and fire three times.

He lets go of my throat, jerking backward. I don't know if all three shots hit him, but I think at least two did. He thrashes around for a minute, then falls still.

In the insanity of the fight, I couldn't hear what happened to Sloane.

All I know is she's not in the room anymore. It's dead silent, other than my own labored breathing.

I don't think she and Remizov passed me—which means there must be a back door out of the dining room.

I'm about to feel my way in that direction when I remember that one of the guards, the one that Sloane hit, was wearing an AR slung over his shoulder.

I feel around on the floor, looking for his body. My hand comes down in a wet patch first, what I think must be blood, until I smell the fermented scent of the wine, and feel the bottle tipped over on its side. That must be what Sloane threw. I find the guard's body next, slumped over close to the table. He's still breathing, but he's going to have a hell of a hangover from that wine.

I get his rifle, slinging it over my own shoulder instead. Then I try to find my way to the back exit, following the table the length of the room, and then feeling along the wall until I find the doorknob.

Once outside the dining room, I can see a little better, as the windows to the outside let in a small amount of moonlight. I find myself at the base of a staircase leading up to the second floor.

Before I've taken two steps toward it, someone starts shooting at me, the bullets whipping so close past my ear I can almost feel the heat. I duck down and press myself against the wall, trying to figure out where the shots are coming from.

A sleek, modern urn explodes next to me. I scramble up into the staircase instead.

I know where the shots are coming from now—two more goons down the end of the hallway.

I take the rifle down off my shoulder and pull the rod back to chamber a round. I flip off the safety and bring the butt of the gun up to my shoulder.

I'm waiting for the guards to come down the hallway. They probably aren't sure if they hit me, or if I ran up the stairs.

I hear the footsteps of one guard, but I know there were two of them. I keep waiting. Sure enough, I hear the second one scuffling out after his colleague.

Once they're both out from cover, I round the corner of the staircase and shoot them both. The first one falls straight to the floor. The second one fires off three more rounds as he falls, but they shoot harmlessly up into the ceiling.

I hear a lot more gunfire coming from outside. I know that's got to be Dom storming the house, though I told him not to do it. His orders were to cut the power if he could, then get Zima out again.

But I have to admit, I'm grateful he didn't listen. From the sounds of it, without the distraction outside, I'd have a dozen more men piling in on me.

I don't know how long Dom will be able to hold them off. I hope he's smart enough to get out when they get too close and not get pinned down anywhere.

I don't know how many more men might be inside, besides the five I've incapacitated. So I have to creep up the staircase slowly, clearing each bend with the AR at the ready, though I'm desperate to run up the stairs full speed to find Sloane.

Remizov's house isn't nearly as large as the monastery, but it's big enough. Once I'm up to the second level, I have no idea which way to go. Until I see a scattering of tiny beads gleaming in the dim light. Dark red, like tiny droplets of blood. Torn from Sloane's dress.

I stalk through the reading room, silent as a panther.

And then I catch sight of them through the French glass doors, standing out on the balcony.

I approach slowly, the rifle up on my shoulder, pointed directly at Remizov.

I push through the doors.

Remizov is standing a dozen yards away, his back against the balcony railing. With the AR I could hit him from three hundred yards, even in the dim light. But he's holding Sloane directly in front of him with a gun pointed at her ribs.

I can see he's disappointed I'm alive. Sloane is the exact opposite. Her relief is palpable. If I didn't know it was impossible, I might even think those were tears sparkling in her eyes.

She doesn't cry out this time, however. She knows our situation has hardly improved.

"Let go of her," I say to Remizov. "I'll put down the rifle. I came here for Sloane—I don't give a shit about killing you."

A few days ago, I wanted revenge on Remizov more than anything in the world.

But now, if I can just walk out of here with Sloane safe and alive, that's the only thing that matters.

Remizov, however, has no intention of letting go of his shield.

He's only an inch or two taller than Sloane. Standing directly behind her, there's no way I can shoot him without hitting her as well.

He wants to wait this out.

He can hear the sounds of the firefight down in the yard as well as I can. If his men win, they'll come up here and riddle me with bullets. If they lose, he can still shoot Sloane before I kill him.

Either way, I'm fucked.

I can see Sloane making the same calculation.

She's running through our options exactly as I am. They are limited in the extreme.

I see her wide, dark eyes looking into mine, trying to communicate everything we've haven't had a chance to say to each other yet.

I want to tell her that I love her. That I want her to stay with me always.

I think she feels the same.

Sloane is the other half of me, my perfect match. I understand her, and she understands me.

So I know what she's thinking when she glances down at the automatic rifle nestled against my shoulder. This is a Ruger AR

556 with armor-piercing rounds. It could go through a Kevlar vest at this range.

Remizov is just a little taller than Sloane. His chest a little higher behind hers.

She looks down at the rifle and back up to my face again.

She gives me the slightest of nods.

The idea is insane.

But I trust her. And she trusts me.

I raise the barrel of the rifle.

Remizov understands what's about to happen right as I start to pull the trigger.

He tries to lift his gun, to shoot me before I can fire.

He's too late.

I aim and shoot. Right through Sloane's shoulder, just below the collarbone. Directly into Remizov's heart.

Sloane slumps to her knees, her hand pressed against her chest.

Remizov tumbles backward off the balcony.

I drop the gun and sprint toward her. I tear off my shirt, ball it up, press it against the exit wound on her back.

I pick her up in my arms.

Her face is white with pain, but she's lucid.

"Nice shot," she says.

I feel like I might have just made the worst mistake of my life. I'm running back through the house, down the stairs, and then out the front door with Sloane in my arms.

I've completely forgotten about the fight on the grounds. When two men run toward me, I'm worse than helpless. But then I recognize Dom and Efrem. Efrem is bleeding from a wound on the arm, but Dom's in one piece.

"How many people did you bring?" I demand furiously.

"All of them, you idiot," Dom says. "You're welcome."

No time to fight about it right now.

"Where's the car?" I say.

Dom takes one look at Sloane. She still has her hand pressed against her shoulder, but the blood is leaking out, running down her arm.

"I'll get it," Dom says, running off across the yard.

"Did anyone else get shot?" I ask Efrem.

"Jasha took one in the leg," he says. "But nobody's dead."

"Good," I say. I'm relieved, or at least I know I should be relieved. But I can't feel anything but terror until I know Sloane is alright.

Dom roars up in his SUV, kicking gravel across our feet.

Efrem opens the back door and I get inside with Sloane still in my arms.

Dom speeds toward the hospital, taking corners so fast that all four wheels are barely staying on the road.

I'm trying to stroke Sloane's hair, trying to comfort her.

She looks up at me, still smiling a little.

"Thanks for coming to get me," she says.

"I'll always come for you," I tell her. "I love you, Sloane."

I've never said those words in my life. Not to anyone.

"I love you, too," she says, tilting up her chin to kiss me.

"Have you ever said that before?" I ask her.

She laughs.

"No," she says. "I never have. But I like it."

"Me too," I say.

I kiss her again.

"Wait," she says, pulling back. "I have to ask you one thing."

"What is it?"

"Did you kill that guy who looked like a linebacker?"

"The one with the smirk?"

"Yes!"

"Oh yeah, I shot him."

"Good," she says, nodding with satisfaction. "I hated that guy."

"What was his deal? He was worse than Remizov."

"Seriously."

Sloane laughs, and then winces. The shirt pressed against her back is almost soaked through.

"Hurry, Dom," I say to my brother.

"We're almost there," Dom says.

I kiss Sloane again, because she can't go anywhere as long as I'm kissing her.

# 25

## SLOANE

For the week I'm stuck in the hospital, Ivan visits me every day. He'd stay all day and all night long if the nurses would let him.

When he does have to leave, he brings Volya to keep watch over me. Volya curls up on the foot of my bed and won't move an inch. He's so massive and fierce looking that the nurses wouldn't dare kick him out. But just like Ivan, he's a sweetheart.

Dom comes to visit as well, and Efrem and Maks. Even Zima comes to eat all the chocolates everybody else has been bringing me.

I always wanted a brother. Now I have too many to count.

And I have something else—a man who makes my heart clench up every time he walks in the room. A man who makes me desperately want to get the bandage off my shoulder so he'll stop worrying about me and ravage my body like a wild animal again.

Ivan said we don't have to talk shop until I'm healed, but of course I've been pestering him for every detail of the aftermath with Remizov.

We scheme and plan together for hours.

We're not giving back one bit of territory to the families who made deals with Remizov. All that belongs to us now.

We've given a cut to the Markovs though. And we've given the whole diamond district to Alter Farkas.

Loyalty should be rewarded.

The first stories have started to come out in the *Gazeta*. St. Petersburg is in uproar about it. The governor seems to be wriggling out of trouble, but the commissioner may have to resign.

Nobody seems to have realized the source of the leaks. They probably think Remizov set the information to release in the event of his untimely demise.

I'm enjoying the chaos. I'm no angel myself, but I can still appreciate when villains get their comeuppance.

Still, I'm itching to leave the hospital and get home to the monastery. I tell Ivan that if he doesn't make the doctor sign me out immediately, I'm going to climb out the window.

Ivan packs up all my things, including the ridiculous number of books and treats he brought for me, and then he whistles for Volya.

Volya stays sitting at the foot of the bed until I give him a pat and say, "Come on, boy."

"What's this?" Ivan says in mock outrage to the dog. "You traitor."

Volya ignores him, trotting along beside me and licking my hand.

"I don't blame him," Ivan says, leaning over to kiss me. "I feel exactly the same."

I walk through the hospital doors, taking a deep breath of the clean winter air.

It's colder and snowier than ever outside.

Still, I stop and stand under the thick falling flakes, thrilled to be outside again.

Ivan wraps his arms around me to keep me warm.

The snow settles in his dark hair, on the shoulders of his wool coat.

The street has that incredible silence that only comes from a thick blanket of snow.

Ivan presses his lips against mine, his mouth warmer than a summer's day, even in the dead of winter.

"Come home, my love," he says.

As we drive up to the monastery, it does feel like home. More than any place I've lived before.

Ivan takes my hand and leads me upstairs. I think he's going to take me straight to the bedroom, but instead he pulls me into the library.

He's set up a table in here, with two chairs and dozens of candles all around. There's a rosebud in a vase atop the linen tablecloth and two formal place settings.

"What's this?" I ask him.

"The night I was going to pick you up at the train station, I wanted to take you out for dinner," he says. "I wanted to take you on a real date."

I can't help laughing.

"We really haven't been on a date, have we?" I say.

"I hope this counts," Ivan says.

He pulls out my chair for me so I can sit down.

He takes the seat across from me.

His face looks unbearably handsome in the glow of the candle-light. I can hardly look at him. Yet, I never want to look at anything else.

He takes my hand across the table.

He pulls a little box out of jacket and places it between us.

My heart is fluttering against my ribs. My fingers tremble as I lift the lid.

I see a gold band, set with a dark green stone.

I take the ring from the box and slip it on my finger. It fits perfectly.

"You're mine forever, my little love," Ivan says. "My own grim reaper."

**Want a little more Ivan & Sloane?** →

Ivan wants to convince Sloane to set a wedding date, but his stubborn little fox won't agree. So he makes a wager she can't refuse...

GET THE BONUS SCENE → GENI.US/BONUS-IVAN

*Warning: Contains some wild and kinky hi-jinx in the gymnasium!*

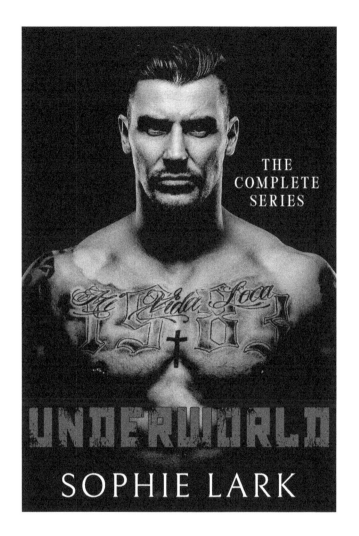

★★★★★ *"The heroes are Alpha males, the women are strong and fierce. Each story is set in a different location, with a unique plot and obstacles to overcome... Scorching hot! So intense and entertaining you won't be able to put them down."*

*"Underworld" is an action-packed, supremely sexy romance series, full of thieves, detectives, mafia princesses, and Bratva bad boys.*

*Each book is a stand-alone and can be read independently. However, if you read in order, you'll find hidden connections to make the story even more fun. There's no cheating or cliff hangers, but there are plenty of spicy scenes, including rough sex and spanking.*

**8 Book Boxset**

**Free Kindle Unlimited**

Download → geni.us/lark-underworld

# THE HEIR
## SOPHIE LARK

# THE REBEL
## SOPHIE LARK

# THE BULLY
## SOPHIE LARK

# THE SPY
## SOPHIE LARK

WELCOME TO KINGMAKERS!
WHERE THERE IS ONLY ONE RULE...


THE HEIR – MARCH 2021
LEO GALLO (SON OF SEBASTIAN & YELENA)


THE REBEL – MAY 2021
MILES GRIFFIN (SON OF CALLUM & AIDA)


THE BULLY – JUNE 2021
DEAN YENIN (SON OF ADRIAN YENIN)


THE SPY – JULY 2021
\*\*\*\*\*\*\*\*\*\* (SON OF \*\*\*\*\*)


KINGMAKERS SERIES PAGE


SOME CHARACTERS FROM MY UNDERWORLD SERIES WILL BE BACK
AS WELL . . .

## WHO'S YOUR NEXT BOOK BOYFRIEND?

CALLUM – BRUTAL PRINCE

MIKO – STOLEN HEIR

NERO – SAVAGE LOVER

DANTE – BLOODY HEART

RAYLAN – BROKEN VOW

SEBASTIAN – HEAVY CROWN

SERIES PAGE – BRUTAL BIRTHRIGHT

CAN I ASK YOU A HUGE FAVOR?

**Would you be willing to leave me a review?**

I would be so grateful as one positive review on Amazon is like buying the book a hundred times. Your support is the lifeblood of Indie authors and provides us with the feedback we need to give the readers exactly what they want!

I read each and every review. They mean the world to me! So thank you in advance, and happy reading!

CLICK TO REVIEW

*Amazon Bestselling Author*

Sophie lives with her husband, two boys, and baby girl in the Rocky Mountain West. She writes intense, intelligent romance, with heroines who are strong and capable, and men who will do anything to capture their hearts.

She has a slight obsession with hiking, bodybuilding, and live comedy shows. Her perfect day would be taking the kids to Harry Potter World, going dancing with Mr. Lark, then relaxing with a good book and a monster bag of salt and vinegar chips.

## The Love Lark Letter
CLICK HERE TO JOIN MY VIP NEWSLETTER

## COME JOIN ALL THE FUN:

## Rowdy Reader Group
THE LOVE LARKS READER GROUP

## Follow for Giveaways
FACEBOOK SOPHIE LARK

## Instagram
@SOPHIE_LARK_AUTHOR

## Complete Works on Amazon
FOLLOW MY AMAZON AUTHOR PAGE

## Follow My Book Playlists
SPOTIFY → GENI.US/LARK-SPOTIFY
APPLE MUSIC → GENI.US/LARK-APPLE

## Feedback or Suggestions for new books?
Email it to me: SOPHIE@SOPHIELARK.COM

Made in the USA
Las Vegas, NV
30 January 2023

66501572R00167